Sovereign Nation

CHILD OF THE RESOULUTION

SHAKA JASPER

Sovereign Nation

CHILD OF THE RESOULUTION

SHAKA JASPER

Wandering Brothers Publishing

Library of Congress Cataloging –in-Publication Data
Jasper, Shaka A.
        Sovereign Nation: Child of the ReSoulution by Shaka
Jasper
                p.   cm.

FIRST PRINTING: JULY 2011

ISBN: 0-9724917-3-2

PRINTED IN THE UNITED STATES OF AMERICA

Wandering Brothers Publishing

WWW.WANDERINGBROTHERS.COM

ACKNOWLEDGEMENTS

FIRST AND FOREMOST, I want to give praise to God. I want to thank God for choosing me to be the vessel to relay his message of friendship and love. I thank God for lifelines of ancestors who built the bridge of life that allowed me to walk the face of this earth and give praise.

I want to thank my mother, Glinda and father, Ralph for following Gods will and providing me with the most precious love there is. I want to recognize and give honor to my father, although I did not have a chance to get to know him personally; the way in which he lived his life resulted in me growing to know and respect his spirit. The stories told to me by family and friends who knew him best constructed my image of him. Thank you for giving me a strong name which has been a great guide for me.

I thank God for my mother, for displaying love through good and challenging times. Thank you for persevering through loss and suffering. Thank you for using your life to show me that family is the most important thing in life and second only to God. Your womanhood encouraged me to be a better man. Thank you for being my greatest cheer-leader throughout my childhood.

I thank God for my family (Grand Parents, Aunts, Uncles,

God Parents and Cousins) for helping my mother to rear me (or raise me as my people will say). Therefore, I can never truly say that I was raised in a single family home. I thank God for my sisters Paresa, Asiunique and Crystal for providing me with a protective love like no other.

I thank God for my brother Ralph, although we have not shared a lot of time together as boys, I look forward to building a foundation of understanding with you as we mature as men. I thank God for the friends I have acquired along this journey of life. For I know that I have taken a piece of you with me.

I thank God for Omega Psi Phi Fraternity, Inc. and for everything I have gained through association. I thank God for the women outside of my bloodline that truly helped me and protected the legacy of my life "My Children".

I thank God for Rose, the mother of my oldest gift from God, my daughter (Destiny Jasper). Thank you for sharing Sydney's love as well. I am honored that she chose to view me as a father. Through all the arguments and misunderstandings you constantly showed me that you will always be a part of my family. Thank you for supporting and protecting our children while I naively faced the challenges of life.

I thank God for Reetu, you provided me the support I needed at the time in which I needed it most. Moreover, through your eyes I was able to gain a better comprehension of the world around and within me. I celebrate the life of your mother; she was a genuinely good and natural woman. My prayers are always with you.

I especially thank God for Natasha, not only did you provide me with my latest gift from God, my child (Eva Jasper); Through the guidance of the Creator you afforded me the freedom I needed to ascend to another level of manhood and grasp the full comprehension of the bond shared between man, woman, child and God. My spirit is always with you.

I dedicate this book to all the righteous souls that had the courage to stand up against tyranny and oppression and laid down their life for love and friendship. To all that read this book, "Greetings to your soul and peace be with you."

PREFACE

OTHER THAN READING THIS BOOK, the only way you will be able to capture the feelings amassed within these pages is to travel back in time to eye-witness a southern lynching or fly to the heavens to have a conversation with the Creator. This is the first novel of a riveting story about an alternate reality for Americans and the friends they share worldwide.

This book represents the genealogy of a chosen child of African-American descent who for some represents a change in the balance of power in America. It showcases the pure heart-felt emotions and thoughts of a neglected generation that grew up during the deconstruction of the American Separatist Era.

Jurist, the main character of the story, provides comprehensible guidance to those who were filtered into prisons and unable to fully assimilate into the perceived American way of life. Jurist is the voice of many post civil rights movement babies who were deprived of the cultural and spiritual guidance of their forefathers and natural mothers due to war, drugs and spiritual deprivation. Because of the capitalization of slavery, a nation once thought of as possessing devout guidance and godly humility is converted into what Jurist believes to be a shadow community covered in criminal apathy and perverse greed.

When Jurist reached his teenage years he is tutored with the understanding that manhood, knowledge and friendship are principles that are essential to his soul. Jurist gains guidance from a long forgotten or better yet hidden group of extremely wealthy corporate elders that seeks to restore their devastated nation of people to its past glory. Faced with heart-break and the burdens of maturity, Jurist crusades to build community alliances while restoring the faith of an embittered people.

To do this Jurist embraces the covenant of his father as he fights historical demons. This is the beginning of the third testament of American-Africans and the ***"ReSoulution of a Sovereign Nation."***

Chapter I
Children's Hero
Year 2042

FOR THE LAST TWENTY YEARS, every August 28th, I've made
a conscious effort to wake up before the sun rises; before the dew
began to settle, and the sky reflected its natural blue hues. As the
day assembles, I grab a book, pen and paper, and walked toward the
grassy flat lands east of the Village of Neter; amongst the beautiful
array of flowers, where the trees stand illuminated by the first rays
of the rising sun, hovering tall and abundant with shade; providing
a place of peace and enlightenment for the soul. Never do I attempt
to stop in my journey; however, on this particular day I decided to
bring with me a group of adolescents who were investigating
historical knowledge.

Their job was to study the challenges and prevailing moments of the
fight for American Africans and the purest form of freedom they
sought. As we sat under the Tree of Enlightenment like Buddha
had done thousands of generation before, we sought wisdom from
the words of our elder W.E.B DuBois by way of the book "The Souls
of Black Folk." Written well over a century ago, "The Souls of Black
Folk" reached beyond its era and speaks of the issues and
challenges we face today.

Reigning from the South, I grew partial to Chapter 9, "Of the Sons
of Masters and Man," a testament of ideas for both blacks and

whites. He challenged Whites to thoroughly examine the problems
of the South, ranging from their orchestrated savage attitudes
towards Blacks, to the growth of an immoral capitalistic society that
thrived on the agricultural economy of the New South.

I will never forget the rush of hopelessness I felt when I first read
his heart as it was written in the pages before me, for it seemed as if
these problems would haunt us as a people forever. Nevertheless,
as I read on, the spirit of the book invigorated me as he discussed
the duties of the trained Negro leaders. His scriptures challenged
all "educated men of skill, men of light and leading, college-bred
men, black captains of industry, and missionaries of culture; men
who thoroughly comprehend and know modern civilization."

As I finished my trip through mental space and time, a child near
the back of the group, a young soul reminiscent of Marcus Garvey
asked emphatically, "Will you tell us the story of Jurist and the
ReSoulution Movement."

My response to her was, "Jurist has no story, for his life was full of
prophecy and truth and friendship affording much more than a
movement.

Most people say the movement for civil rights began hundreds of
years ago. But for Jurist the movement ended and the ReSoulution
began with the timidity he lost when he wrote his first black history
paper in middle school."

"Can I recite the paper," shouted a young warrior-princess draped
in a beautiful white gown. She jumped up from her seating and
rushed to the front of the group when I gladly accepted her offer.
The story of Jurist's black history paper is read to the young like the
scriptures of the Old Testament were read to the Hebrew children
of Israel. Every house within the village has extensive chronological
knowledge of the forthcoming of the New Messiah. Although she
couldn't have been birthed into the world no more than eight or
nine years ago she had already learned hundreds of years of
knowledge.

"Why yes, you may my future queen." I responded to her.

"Thank you GOD-father." She turned to the group and commanded their attention. With the soulful sound of her voice she enticed their intellect by using the drums of their ears to play sounds of ancestral wisdom.

She eloquently narrated Jurist's *Black History Paper:*

"As I look upon the world with clarity, so many variations of me intake the perceptions that precede my many different attitudes and dispositions. I often find myself reminiscing about past events that for the most part were things un-witnessed by my own eyes. Sometimes I despise this hypnotizing wondering within my brain. Do I search for fame, try to entertain, find friends to help me maintain. My speech is often displayed with such profound sound that spreads around like the wind preceding my voice faster than a horse, even the white horse.

Is it my choice to choose between the past that I've never witnessed and the classes that my friends never paid attention to? Too many beings suffer from a visible prison of separateness. I know we have yet to heal because I still feel the pain. The heartfelt lashes I continue to receive when I attempt to dream represent the pain of a forgotten struggle. The fields helped determine our teams. My will is at its lowest point. What is the point? Trinity and peaceful living isn't it enough? Isn't it enough wealth? Isn't it enough gold? Hasn't my labor afforded you thrones? Let me go home! Let me go home!

From my heart I ask you of resembling skin, has your heart gone pale like faces of our culture captors? Is it their fault that we can't trace the place from which we gained our spiritual grace or is it my face that keeps me imprisoned on your estate and away from my ancestral birthplace? Rwanda may have been my home! The job of making sure the master's niggers are all in place have reinstated the mentality of yesterday. Or was yesterday simply a preview of tomorrow.

I live a trans-dimensional life with a predestined purpose and relentless sacrifice, existing through the span of eternal lifelines. For, I died hundreds of years ago and I sit here before you today a ghost, haunting you in your dreams. Aren't you mad you can't get rid of me? I'm an angel of God in any form I choose. For now, I am the word for which you are in tuned. Look at how I am determining your mood. Acknowledge the many ways my words move you. Sit back and let God school you. Groove to my sound; better yet repent with me now.

Show me how! Tell me now! How many of your sons and daughters will you watch cry because my intelligence blinds you as I walk by, with my head up high, as they sit idly and face down? Go ahead try. Wipe your eyes and explain to them why I can get in now. Show them our past and ask for their forgiveness because history shall show them how they came to inherit the statistical and economical advantage.

Isn't it strange how that ghost that you thought was lost at sea keeps returning to say hi, so nice, so polite? Not like the beast of the days that use to impede our mothers and fathers path to freedom. Now ya'll wonder selfishly if yesterday's heathens want a piece of what ya'll stole; and continue to steal: if you don't believe me look towards the Black Hills. Hell nall, keep your devils gold. I only need the trees to mold my home. Let our knees be the thrones that make our children feel like royalty. But you expect us to have loyalty.

Since when did we become your measuring rods for charity? Forcefully, you fornicated with my great-grand mother outside of marriage and without her consent. Not a tear from her eyes could wash away the despair from her heart. You raped Goddesses and murdered Mother Nature. You sucked from her breast and pressed upon her lips and it all began with a staining rip; resulting in fear and terror, terror of the deeds that come in the falsified name of God. How long must we wait for the great

affliction to finish. When will this obsession of inferiority vanquish and the fears of evolution diminish.
How many colors do you see?

As we continue on this journey of life, our comprehension grows as each day passes by. We all fly towards the heavens. But suddenly like a spectrum in the sky, I veer 41 degrees away from these routine beings, drawn towards the rainbow of fearless souls along the way.

To be honest I'm not sure if I want to share this truth with you today, for fear that your mind is still in bondage and not ready to be freed. Hesitation is in my psyche yet freedom is in my soul. "Blessed are they that readth, and they that hear the words of this prophecy, and keep those things that are written therein, for the time is at hand." One should base one's life on faith not fear; therefore I know that the hour to free all minds is near.

Our ancestors freed our bodies and left us the blueprint to free our souls. I have studied the ways of the world for almost 26,000 years, yet still I possess only little known knowledge that's worth more than my weight in gold. But I know if we work together we can find the pathway to the land of the lord and free the souls of our beloved ancestors who were once called GODS. For freeing their souls should be our fundamental goal.

Now what I'm sharing with you can be proven or disproved by any scientific, philosophical, or religious book. However, I am going to use the bible of our ancestral kin, the unwritten book of "common sense" again and again, for it is the only book that we ever needed to use (although Exodus was the chapter that our ancestors knew to choose). Therefore Jurist Isaiah Johnson became my full name, read it right to left like our Muslim kin and it reveals a great prescience hidden within English slang, "Johnson-the first slave, Isaiah-son Jehovah has favored, Jurist-with knowledge of the law" and I'm telling ya'll like Mrs. Sealy told Harpo, "You'll never have nothing, till you do right by me." So, now it's time that all minds are set free.

5

"Sojourner, tell it again!" A child from the front of the group shouted. Then one of the older adolescents cries out, "No, we want to hear the whole story." Then the rest of the group converged in agreement with the older adolescent, "Yeah, tell the whole story GOD-Father," they all screamed in unison.

I was a youthful, old man when I lead that group of kids to the century old Bo tree and gave in to their collaborated request for me to tell them the story of Jurist Isaiah Johnson, "The Child of the ReSoulution."

"All right, All right I'll tell ya'll, but the only way you can truly grasp this ancestral truth is if you know the whole truth. And since we have to hurry back for the feast, I don't want to hear one single interruption."

 "Okay!" With smiled that would equal the length of the mouth of the Nile River if combined, they all nodded in agreement.

Chapter 2
Three Nations

*Circumspectly, I am that nigga, who refuses to accept your false
doctrines fed to us on a toxic spoon.
The nigga that cares less about your personal views regarding
him and what he chooses.
Resolutely, I am the nigga that will never exchange the lives of the
past, present and future to placate your superficial soul.
Infinitely, I am that nigga, taking mental pictures of your world
and break it down for little boys and girls.
Never folding, I am that nigga, enslaved by laborers of a nation,
victim to its own greed.
Survival of the fittest explains the theoretic relationship between
neighboring beings.
By the way, socialist unity is the only remedy for this elitist
mentality instilled in this reverently niggarish King.
Relentlessly, I am that nigga, still trying to break free.
"Shuhs, Shuhs"
"Here comes the master and he's with Tom & Uncle Sam."
"Hurry up nigga run."
"Tom, where's that nigger that's causing so much trouble for me?"
"That's him Master as Black as he can be!"
"Yes, I am that nigga."
And I am Free!*

"IT WAS THE EARLY 1960'S, IN THE 'DIRTY SOUTH,' and during those times, Whites didn't have to mask their prejudice attitudes with a glossy layer of affirmative action make-up. No, no, no, it was nothing like today. The lines were drawn on every water fountain, every school, every church, every home, and every business. Everything was the way God wanted it to be. There were clearly three separate nations for people of African descent; whites, coloreds, and Niggers; although, Coloreds and Niggers were basically the same. Whites were perceived to be intellectually and morally superior. Coloreds were submissive, ingratiating, and didn't oppose the state of affairs. But those niggers you see, they were a problem from the start.

Whites hated niggers because they would cause trouble in every city they visited. I say visited because niggers were never permitted to stay for extended periods of time. For if they attempted to stay and not adapt to the passive good-natured standards of the colored people; they would surely face serious consequences. Punishment for a nigger could range from a simple cross being set ablaze in front of a house as fair warning, to the complete destruction of a colored/nigger community. Therefore, it swiftly became very important for all coloreds to decide which of the two they would preferably become. Nevertheless, more and more coloreds became niggers.

Niggers started spreading everywhere like a plague, provoking and enticing previously well-mannered coloreds to assemble with them, develop innovative ideas, and collective ways to improve the quality of living for people of African descent. Before the Whites knew it, the majority of their obedient, well-behaved, congenial coloreds (by their standards) had been converted into disrespectful, resourceful, tenaciously deceitful niggers. But in the community of people of African descent, to be a colored person that wanted to bring about change in the South, one had to become what was coined a "Revolutionary."

Revolutionaries and niggers were all the same, in the eyes of the

Whites, and coloreds had to descend from his or her status of being colored and disgrace his or herself to that of a no good nigger if he or she even contemplated Revolutionary thoughts.

Back in the days, both coloreds and niggers had certain rules they had to abide by whenever they exited their homes; especially if they were traveling outside their community. These rules were called the "Three Rules of a Traveler."

Chapter 3
Three Rules of a Traveler

IT'S A MIDSUMMER DAY OF THE EARLY NINETEEN SIXTIES and a heat wave is passing through the southern city of Atlanta, GA. Hot winds are blowing dusts of red clay, while scores of children are playing, skipping, and jumping rope to the beats of penny loafers and quarter-inched heels marching down the sidewalk throughout downtown. That's why Pharaoh decided to stay the night at David's home. They thought it would be best if they stayed together, woke up had a good breakfast and then got on the road to go to the March. They felt so alive and invigorated. In fact, they felt so enthused, they stayed up longer than expected exchanging thoughts and ideas about the rally, and they weren't able to wake up on time.

"Y'all boys betta wake up in there."

"Ma, it's too early to be gettin up." David responds without even openings his eyes to see the sunlight and birth of a new day.

"David, you betta get yo behind up and come eat before this food gets cold," Mrs. Conan screamed in a voice more thunderous than before. "Besides, your daddy is waiting for y'all at the church, so get up. "Today is a very important day and I know you and Pharaoh don't want me to have to come back there." She yells!

Although Mrs. Conan was a beautiful, short and slender woman with long, sleek jet-black hair that she obviously got from the Native American side of her family, she could fill a house with a single scream and make you think that she was six feet tall and weighed 180 pounds.

"Here we come, Mrs. Conan," Pharaoh responds.

"David, get up!

"Where are the towels?"

David and Pharaoh were like night and day. David was an average size young man, a skillful mathematician with a laid back attitude. He was the color of a fine piece of toast with skin as smooth as butter. David was very outspoken in public, well versed with a socialist demeanor. Pharaoh on the other hand was a slender, well-trimmed dark child who relied on his street smarts and his ability to perceive situations and people. He was also a strong young man with the attributes of a well-trained athlete and he probably could be a high school All-American if he was to ever try-out for a sport. But Pharaoh viewed athletics as a gateway to modern day institutional slavery; he would never court the idea of becoming an athlete; he hated the entire sporting arena. Instead, he chose debating. Pharaoh constantly worked on refining his speech, his etiquette, and the way he listened. Nonetheless, David was a sports fanatic, especially track and field events, where blacks were really able to display their seemingly genetic dominance. The difference of interests didn't hinder the bond or the level of friendship that these young brothers constantly displayed. They were like Batman and Robin with David playing Batman, the older casual brother with the tools of economic stability and a sustainable family nucleus on his side. While Pharaoh played Robin, the self-taught street kid with a lot of potential and only a hand full of broken worn out tools to help him reach his goals.

Hesitant to get up, David told Pharaoh to look in the closet outside the room for the towels.

"Get up man, you forgot we're supposed to go, and help your Dad at the church."

David stretched, "Aw man, what time is it?"

"Time for you to get up."

"Where you going?"

"I'm going to get me something to eat, you didn't hear yo mama?"

"Man, I was dreaming that we were at the march, and Dr. King came out and asked me to come up on the stage with him."

"I mean it was beautiful man."

"We stood in front of everybody."

"We could see damn near every black woman and man in America and it was beautiful."

"You talking crazy now, I'm fixin to go and get me something to eat."

Pharaoh walked out of David's room, down the hall, and into the bathroom. He closed the door, and flips the light switch to give him a little extra light. He then reached in a little closet, and pulled out a face towel, and turned towards the sink. But before he turned the water on, he stared at himself in the mirror, and started reciting, "You will be a great man; you will be a great man."

"Come on man," David pounded on door, "What's taking you so long in there?"

Pharaoh slowly snapped back to reality, turned on the water, and hollered, "I'll be out in a minute."

When Pharaoh finishes washing his face, he opened the door and looked down at David who is standing in the doorway.

"I thought you were in a rush," said David sarcastically.

"You just hurry up little man," Pharaoh, whispered as passing.

Growing impatient with both the boys, Mrs. Conan urges them both to hurry, come to the kitchen so they can eat, and leave.

"Ya'll boys know better. Ya'll best be gettin on that road today. That's why I told ya'll not to go to sleep so late. David, your father has been waiting on you at the church ever since seven o'clock this morning."

"Ma, it's only eight o'clock."

"Yeah, and before you know it, it will be nine o' clock and time for Saturday school. Now hurry up and eat your food."

David and Pharaoh finished their food and took their bags out to the car. While loading their suitcases in the trunk, they noticed an unfamiliar sparkling, powder-blue Pontiac riding by. Pharaoh was the first to spot it, so he taps David who is leaning into the trunk trying to make room for everything. "Hey, David look, who is that?"

"Who's who," David responds. Pharaoh points to the car trying not to look too obvious.

"Them!"

"I don't know, but it looked like they're going over to Mrs. Brown house."

"Did you see the girl in the passenger seat?"

"N'all, how she look?"

"Like a beauty queen."

"Did you boys pack something to eat?" Mrs. Conan yells from the screen door. But before she could go back in the house, she spots Mrs. Tisha Brown coming outside to greet her guest. "Hey, Tisha. How you doing?"

Mrs. Brown responds, "Fine girl, why don't you come over and I'll introduce you to my sister-in-law and niece."

"I'll be there in a minute let me finish packing these boy's a lunch for the road."

Mrs. Conan walked back into the house to prepare the boys lunch. Meanwhile, David and Pharaoh are still waiting for the girl to get out. Then out of nowhere, David yells, "Mrs. Brown can I help you all with anything?"

"Why, yes you can," David closed the trunk, and told Pharaoh to 'come on,' as he dashes across the street.

"What you want us to do Mrs. Brown?"

"Can you boys help them grab their bags out of the trunk and put them in the guest room for me please?"

"No problem."

As they pass by the passenger side of the car Pharaoh glanced in at the girl on the passenger side. In that moment it was if the sun and the moon had taken a break because time stood still for Pharaoh. In less than a minute Pharaoh pictured them spending an eternity together. It was if they were under a tree in the forest of love with her lying in his lap peeling fruit as he spoke words of truth that sounded like poetry.

"Although my mind thinks it is flaw my heart knows it is real, this

attraction I feel. Much similar to the magnetism between the Earth and the Moon, how together they can bring about beautiful tides or astonishing typhoons, which create waves that penetrate time linking lifelines that usually remain undisturbed because they exist in different but parallel worlds. Yet, as we wonder through time individually, inevitably we have reached the time where our paths must cross, compelling us to seek for more time together. Forcing us to think about times, we are together and times we are apart. Nevertheless, this is how it starts, like a plotted course on a chart, to locate the twinkle of an allusive star."

Then just like that the booming sound of Nandi's mother snatches Pharaohs attention from the haven of his dream back to reality.

"Nandi, will you turn off that music and help grab some of this stuff out the car?"

Back from his dream Pharaoh asked, "How you doing Ma'am? What do you want us to get first?"

"How you doing boys, I'm Mrs. Brown sister-in-law, Mrs. Grant, and that's my daughter Nandi, inside the car. Nandi, this is the last time I'm going to tell you to get out of the car and help with these bags. Most of them belong to you anyway. I don't know why you packed so much stuff in the first place you're only going to be here for the summer.

As the boys grab a couple of suitcases out of the trunk Nandi steps out of the car. "Ma, they're playing my favorite song on the radio. You know I can't get out until it's finished."

"Girl, you bout to get on my last nerve! You better get out that car before I knock you into the middle of next week."

"Hello!" Mrs. Conan walked up. "I brought you all a sweet potato pie. I baked it last night."

"That's so sweet of you, Hi I'm Jenny Grant. I'm married to Tisha's brother James."

"Excuse me Mrs. Brown which way is the guest room," David asked.

"Ya'll boys just follow me. I appreciate ya'll help. So, where ya'll boys bout to go off to."

"We about to go to the March in Atlanta," David told her.

Nandi's head turned in the direction of the boys, as the mentioning of the march catches her attention.

"Ya'll boys make sure you be careful, them white folks ain't playing up there. You can just sit those bags right there by the dresser baby. I'm sorry I didn't get your name." She asked as she looked over to Pharaoh.

"Pharaoh, Ma'am."

"Pharaoh, that's a mighty, strong name! David you can put them by the foot of the bed. Pharaoh, no wonder you want to go up to the march. What's your last name?"

"Johnson."

"You ain't related to Avery Johnson from 31st street are you?"

"Yes Ma'am, that's my father."

You could tell from the expression on her face that she knew Pharaoh's father personally because of the way her cheek bones started to rise, and the giddy demeanor her face postured.

"Me and your father went to school together. That was a fine man and he could he play some ball. That boy was a born athlete. It's a shame that he got caught by those clansmen that night: him and Bobby Jones. But at least he was able to get away, although I don't see how; after all, he did get shot in the leg. So, how is ol' speedy doing? I haven't seen him in about fifteen years."

"I guess he's all right; I haven't seen him that much lately."

"Well, Mrs. Brown we need to get going," David intervened before the situation became too odd for Pharaoh, "We got to go and meet my dad at the church."

"Ya'll boys be safe, I'll keep ya'll in my prayers."

"David, Pharaoh, ya'll come here," Mrs. Conan called out to the boys while standing by the car with Mrs. Grant, "Here is ya'll lunch! Now ya'll hurry up, and get to the church. Moses is waiting on ya'll. Now both of ya'll give me a hug, and be safe. I love you!"

"'Bye Mrs. Conan, and it was nice meeting you all as well," Pharaoh said as he waves to the women, while looking at young Nandi.

"Hey Pharaoh, are you going to ask her can you get it back?" David asked with a conniving smirk on his face.

"Get what back, I didn't leave anything"

"I don't know about that. It looked to me like you left both your eyes, and your heart, back there with Nandi."

"Man I was just looking."

David and Pharaoh open the doors of the car and get in.

"Yeah, you were looking all right. If you would have looked any harder you would've been able to look right through her."

"Negro, be quiet and crank up the car. We need to hurry up and get to the church. Your daddy is waiting for else."

"All right, I'll cool out right now, but when we get on the road I'll start back up."

"Well, I need to stay here then; if you going to be running your mouth about nonsense the entire way there."

"See look, now you don't even want to go you so ready to get back and look at Nandi."

"Boy will you just shut up and drive! I'm not thinking about that girl; besides, she's here for the summer," Pharaoh said with excitement and playfulness.

As soon as David and Pharaoh arrived at the church, they could hear David's father yelling, "Go grab the chairs out the backroom and put them in order."

David whispered to Pharaoh, "Man we haven't even gotten out of the car and he already wants us to go to work."

"Just come on, the quicker we finish, the faster we'll be able to leave and go to the march," Pharaoh, calmly suggests."

"Yeah and the quicker you can get back to Nandi."

"All right, that's it, now you get to taste a couple of knuckle sandwiches."

David then made a mad dash into the church where he knew Pharaoh would spare him. After the boys finished arranging the chairs, Mr. Conan called out to them. David rushed over to his father's side, and feels compelled to explain his tardiness.

"Dad, I'm sorry we were late, we just wanted to..." but before David could finish his sentence, Pharaoh looked at him with condemning eyes, as if to say leave him out of his excuse. It was as if they used telepathy to communicate with one another; immediately after he looked at Pharaoh, he stopped including Pharaoh in his excuse. "I mean, I needed a little more rest and then we had to help Mrs. Grant."

Walking pass David, Mr. Conan seemed to disregard David's excuse for being late, "Save your excuses son, I have something more important I want to share with you. Ya'll boys follow me."

David and Pharaoh followed Mr. Conan into his office. Then Mr. Conan looked back and asked Pharaoh to close his office door. Pharaoh quickly turned around, pulled the door shut and locked it. David then walked over to his father's desk and sat down in the only seat that's in front of the old, dry mahogany desk. Although David pays little attention to the old desk, Pharaoh looked at it and wondered how many confessions that old desk had witnessed and how many tears had it soaked into its very fiber. As he glanced around the room, Pharaoh noticed the many pictures of Christ and his disciples. He found it strange that although there were no portraits, or pictures, of Christ within the embodiment of the church, Mr. Conan would however have portraits of a Black version of Christ and his disciples within his private chamber. For a quick minute, he pondered whether or not he should ask Mr. Conan if he thought Jesus was Black. But his thoughts were soon interrupted by a flashback story of Mr. Conan.

"David, Pharaoh I want both of you to listen very carefully to what I am about to tell you. When I was a young man we went through some very tough times. Back then we stayed back in the woods of the small community that later became known as Sweet Auburn. Sometimes alone, I would have to walk ten or twenty miles to find work. One day I met this traveler; that day is so clear. He was a small man with a reddish complexion. He dressed like the woods and he smelled like he stayed in them as well. You could tell that Mr. Conan was visualizing what happened because he started leaning back in his chair and began to slowly rock. "He told me that his name was Spirit Guider. I remember that day so clearly because he asked me a question that I continued to ask myself every day since."

"What did he ask dad?" David quickly intervened.

19

"If you keep quiet long enough, I'll tell you." Mr. Conan paused a moment and stared at his son. "He asked, what do you think would happen to your family if you didn't come back?"

"It took me a while to answer his question because I'd never thought about that before. After much deliberation I told him that they would probably starve."

That's when he said, "That's a pretty heavy weight to carry for such a young boy."

Then he asked, "What is your name?" Apprehensively I replied to him, "Moses, Moses Conan." He then asked me."

"Moses, is this your first time traveling through these woods alone?"

"In a solemn voice I answered him, Yes sir."

"Well, this is your lucky day, young Moses. I have a present for you."

"As he reached in his bag, I didn't know whether to smile and stay or turn and run."

"This is a precious gift because it will help keep you safe as you walk through the shadows."

"Anxiously I prepared my hands for a gift and my legs for a mad dash just in case there was trickery." He stood upright and said, "They're called the Three Rules of a Traveler."

"Rules," I thought to myself, "How can three rules be considered a gift?"

"Rule one," he said, "Always show worship to your god before you leave a destination and pray for the ones you love. Rule two, make a map of where you are traveling and plot your stops. Rule number three, always remember to carry a big stick to help you when you are in need. Have you done either of the first two because I can see that you don't have a stick?"

"My response to him was, my mama and I prayed together before I left, but no I didn't plot my way and I don't have a stick. But I know which way I need to go."

"Moses, sometimes even the right way can be the wrong way. Here, take this map I made of the northern part of the woods and this is a staff. It may be too big for you now, but I have the feeling that one day it will be the right size. Then I heard a noise behind me that made me turn my head and in an instant Spirit Guider was gone."
"Dad you sure you didn't dream this after laying down on a rock for too long."

"Boy didn't I tell you to listen. Then that mean I don't want to hear you talk."

"Yes Sir."

Mr. Conan walked to a closet and reached all the way to the back of it behind a stack of old books, and pulled out a long wave shaped stick. "You see, this was all we had for protection when we traveled because if you got caught carrying a gun around in those times you either stole it or you were a troublemaker and for participating in either offense you would more than likely be beaten and possibly hanged."

"Dad, did you really believe that stick was going to protect you if they really wanted to hang you?
"He still here ain't he." Sarcastically, Pharaoh answered him.
"Thank you Pharaoh." Mr. Conan graciously responds. "But times have changed and like all things we change to fit our environment, therefore I am going to give you boys this."

Mr. Conan reached back into the closet and grabbed a riffle. David eyes became as wide and bright as a deer caught in the headlights of an oncoming car.

"I thought you said never to touch it unless we were going hunting."
"I know what I said, I'm giving you boys this for protection because
to some people ya'll are the prey. Now come here, let's pray and
plot ya'll a course to travel.

Chapter 4
Red Dog Ritual

AFTER RECEIVING THE THREE RULES OF A TRAVELER FROM MR. CONAN, David and Pharaoh made their way to the march in Atlanta. David drove his father's car as Pharaoh painted civil rights posters on the passenger side. Meanwhile, driving in the opposite direction on the same road a couple miles up the road, a drunk driver passes a gas station and knocked down the whites only sign posted by the entrance on the side of the highway. Jokingly, David told Pharaoh, "We're going to have the ugliest posters at the march."

"If you stop running over every bump in the road I'll have it looking like Edward Bannister painted it himself, Pharaoh retorts."
"Yeah and I'm related to Michael Angelo."

"With eyes like yours I highly doubt it. Hey watch out." Pharaoh alerts David, as David swerves off the side of the road barely managing to avoid hitting the dusty red, pick-up truck driven by a reckless, drunk driver.

David regains control of the car and drives back onto the road a little nervous. "Damn, I didn't even notice that honkie."
"You need to pay attention to the road and stop thinking about Ti

Ti."

"I wasn't thinking about that girl."

"Oh she's that girl now. Just the other day, she was a real woman. The type of natural woman a man needs in his life. Isn't that what you said?"

"Whatever man. A moment later David asked, "You hear that?"

"Hear what?"

"That knocking noise."

"Man, you hearing things."

"We need to stop to a gas station."

"For what? I don't hear anything."

"It doesn't matter. We need to get some gas anyway."

Pharaoh protest, "Not from around here, we can't make it to a city? See man, I told you to stop in Valdosta like your daddy said."

"My father's a preacher, he always talks like that, and I don't know if we will make it to another city. What, you so scared of the White man that you want to turn around and go back to a gas station just because my father told you about some wood story."

Pharaoh turned and looked at David with a serious stare and said, "Yelp, and so should you."

"Not as long as I have this I'm not," David replied as he pulled out his father's riffle.

"Put that rifle up before you shoot us both."

"What about that one there, it looked clean." David points to the Red Dog Gas Station.

This happens to be the same gas station that the drunk driver had just passed two miles ago.

"Just because it's White, don't mean it's clean, David."

"Whatever, you don't see a Whites only sign up do you."

David pulled over to the gas station in spite of Pharaoh's concern.

"David you go pump the gas you can give me the money and I'll pay for it while you check for your mysterious noise."

"If I'm paying, why am I pumping?"

Pharaoh answered, "Because I didn't want to stop here in the first place."

"Here's an extra twenty-five cents bring me back a juice too." Pharaoh took the money and walked in the store. But he doesn't see or hear anyone. So he walked around beckoning for service, "Hello, Hello is anyone here? After standing at the counter for a minute he began to walk towards the back wall cooler with the juices in them. He grabbed two grape juices and walk back to the counter. In the meantime, David is under the hood checking the oil and transmission fluids. After a couple minutes of waiting at the counter for the service person to come Pharaoh started screaming, "Hello! Is anyone here? Hello." Pharaoh then spots a bell on the opposite side of the cash register he leaned over and rang the bell and waits a moment then he began to walk down the candy and sweet cake aisle leaving the juice on the counter. "Ain't this a bit..."

Then out of nowhere in a quiet dash, a large white man races up behind Pharaoh and hits him across the head with a bat. Disgusted with the sight of Pharaoh in his store, Jesse (the owner) pulled Pharaoh to the back of the store where he and his friends were sitting and playing checkers. "I don't know why I put a sign up. You niggers just ain't gonna learn how to read anyways."

When Jesse got to the back porch, breathing heavily, he shouted, "Hey fellas look what we got us."

Bubba was the first to respond. "What you got there, Jesse?" He answered as he continues to play.

"I done caught me a nigger! And I got first dibbs this time! "Oh no you don't; you and Bubba already got more than anybody in the county," Willie answered.

Jesse commented, "That's because God chose to reward us for our diligent work in helping him rid our nation of this plague."

Meanwhile, David is sitting in the car growing tired of waiting, "What's taking this Negro so long?"

While David began to exit the car to go to the store, the men in the back of the store started getting Pharaoh, ready. Jesse gags Pharaoh while Bubba holds his arms and Willie ties his legs down with the belt from his pants. Stripped of his pants and unconscious to what's going on. Pharaoh lies on the ground almost motionless. David entered the store and saw Pharaoh nowhere in sight. He then became nervous and scared. "Pharaoh, hey Pharaoh," he whispered. "Damn it!" David rushed out to the car, grabbed the rifle, and sprints back to the store. Upon his re-entry to the store he heard some talking in the back. Nervously, he walked towards the sound and saw a group of men surrounding the seemingly lifeless body of Pharaoh. The feeling of shock and aw rushed through David's body heading straight to his heart as he observes his friend bludgeoned and traumatized by the imminent danger that surrounds him.

"I got your manhood now nigger." Jesse screamed out as he stood over Pharaoh's castrated body. Pharaoh's agony sculptured face falls to his right where he and David stare faithlessly into each other's eyes.

Chapter 5
Pharaoh's Curse

Clouds and mystic thoughts
Slurred voices and hypnotized souls.
Catch me catch me I'm falling into this mind of mine. Oh Lord, Oh
Lord
Hear me hear me as I speak with the voices of time.
Capture my thoughts from this sea of despair.
Cleanse my body with this wisdom in the air.
Bury me in this world of isms.
Where even holy men are placed in satanic prisons,
Senseless demons escort me through this gateway to hell.
Mercenary vengeance dethroned me with flying steel everywhere.
Everywhere I turn they act like they don't care.
In this world of wolves, I must be the hare,
Struggling to survive in a forest that is bare,
Unnerving the tribe by taking away its king.
Dismay has surrounded even my closest human beings.
If today is my last day then let it be the end.
Call out the savages because now GODS become as devilish as
men.

It's the year 1969, in a small agricultural town in South Florida, after the desegregation of the local community high school, Pharaoh

28

prepares to make a speech to the hundreds of individuals that are amongst the crowd.

Pharaoh's Speech:

My people, fear has kept us oppressed for too long. Now we have to make the choice to continue on with our way of life or integrate, assimilate, and ultimately acculturate into the customs, traditions, and behaviors of the masses.

From this day forth, we must preside over our own destiny, lest our unity will be lost within the capitalistic thoughts and nature of this errant nation. No longer can we afford to listen without comprehending, see without observing, or work for a people whose countenance for righteousness runs short. The time has come for us to stand strong in our precepts to take care of our own. Activities that will be conducive to our plight should be the only acceptable deeds achieved by members of our community.

By implementing community-oriented policies, we will be able to police ourselves, recycle and generate our own currency, and dictate the actions of our children through neighboring-family intervention. Let us not forget the old saying that 'it takes an entire village to raise a child.' We must rekindle our knowledge of old to reestablish a culture that reflected the ingenuity, intellect, and self-sacrificing nature of our ancestors. Their laws are exactly what they are, their laws.

Although we are bound by neighborly respect to adhere to their laws, by no means should their laws ever supersede our way of life. Now, not later, now is our chance to formulate such a plan. Many others including myself are willing to form a committee to draft such a unified proposal and this is how the unspoken community will convey its way of life. Progress through Knowledge! Prosperity through Freedom!

Applauds throughout the crowd are suddenly changed to screams and crying. As two shots fired from a near-by building, penetrates the chest of Pharaoh, killing him almost instantly. His wife Nandi, with toddler son Jurist, in her arms watches in disbelief as she instinctively rushed to her husband's side with Jurist still in her arms as she began to scream out her husband's name.

"Pharaoh, Pharaoh, no GOD, please GOD help me, somebody help me. Somebody help meee!"

Soon after the shooting, a small group of men begin to gather and walk through the streets towards the local merchant stores. Then one of the men picked up a rock and stared at the store of this old white man that is known throughout the community to be a racist. One of the guys to his right whispered in his ears do it, I got your back. After that it was nothing else to say. When it all ended 25 people were arrested, 15 people were injured and 2 stores were burned to destruction.

Chapter 6
Regeneration
Twelve years later

JURIST AND NANDI ARE BOTH IN THE KITCHEN. Nandi is washing dishes and talking to Jurist.

"Mama what happened?" He asked in a calm questionable manner. She responded with uncertainty in her voice, "What you mean what happened?"

"To my daddy, who killed him? "I know you don't like to talk about it, but I really would like to know what happened that day."

Nandi turned to Jurist and asked, "Baby, why would you assume that I don't like to talk about your father?"

"No ma, not about my father, I know more about my father than you think I know. I want you to tell me about the day he died. I already know them crackers killed him."

"I don't know who killed him, the police never found a suspect."

"I wish I could find the crackers who did it, I'll show them."

"Show them, show them what Jurist?" Jurist could hear the tension in his mother's voice, "That you can be as vicious and sadistic as some of them can be. And why are you constantly referring to white people as crackers. I never said that you could use that type of language in my house. Only a person that lacks intelligence would resort to using one derogatory word to describe a group of people who are all individually different. Besides, what makes you think that it was some white people who killed your father? Black people can kill just as well as White people."

"Why do you call them White people? Their skin is no more White than mine is Black. Man please!"

"Boy don't you man please me," Nandi's voice grows deeper with more convictions and force, "I'm your mama not some guy off the street. You have been hanging up on that corner too much."

"Ma, how could I not know about my father? Every time somebody realizes who my father is they tell me, 'Boy, your daddy was a good man. He wasn't afraid of nobody, especially not those crackers. That's why they killed him.'"

"All I know is that on that day a great and pure man was taken away from us."

"When I grow up I'm going to be just like my daddy. I'm going to fight for my people but ain't nobody going to kill me. Watch mama, you'll see. I'm going to run this country and so-called black people are going to have the land and the money. Then I'm going to show them (Jurist was about to say cracker but quickly remembers what his mother had just said) so-called White people how it feels to live like me."

"Jurist you can't be like all the mean and hateful people of this world. Your father fought for equal opportunities and the strengthening of our community. He didn't hate white people he hated the situation that was forced upon our people. Let me show you something."

Nandi goes to her closet, and pulled out a gold colored briefcase. She opened it without a key or combination, and looked at several pictures, pamphlets, tapes, letters, and speeches that belonged to Pharaoh.

"Here," she closed the briefcase and hands it over to Jurist, "Your daddy would have wanted you to have this." Maybe it will help you understand him and what he stood for a little better."

Jurist grabbed Pharaoh's briefcase went to his room and immediately began reading every poem and speech that Nandi had saved. He even listened to the speeches that were recorded the day of his father's murder. As Nandi walked in to tell Jurist that his dinner is ready, she saw Jurist in tears listening to the shots being fired and the people screaming and shouting.

In a concerned motherly voice, she asked him, "Baby, are you all right?" Nandi walked over to Jurist and comforts him by putting her arms around him and gently stroking the back of his head as he lays it upon her shoulders. But all Jurist could do was cry. "Go ahead let it out. But baby you have to understand things were different back then. Everyone was marching and boycotting and some people were not comfortable with our efforts to push the Black Rights issue."

"Why didn't he have protection?"

"Your daddy knew his involvement in the movement was dangerous, but he accepted those dangers because he accepted his position in the movement courageously. He once told me that the two went hand and hand. But times have changed now Jurist."
"Yeah, the times have changed but the problems remain the same."

Jurist combats her statement, "He died for nothing." Jurist rose his head up off his mother's shoulder.

Before she knew it, Nandi grabbed Jurist by his shoulders and shook him with a strong force.

"Boy don't you ever let me hear something like that come out your mouth again." Nandi aggressively replied, "Your daddy and our friends assisted the fight to desegregate our schools and supply free food to students who could not afford lunch. Your father's a martyr within this community because he believed that one day things would get better and he was willing to exchange his life for his beliefs."

Jurist got up off the bed and began to walk out the room with a haunting look upon his face, as he asked his mother, "But mama, are things better?"

Chapter 7
Rise of a New Day

JURIST IS WALKING TO SCHOOL when he heard his friend Ermine calling his name. Ermine is a very bright boy that comes from an integrated family. His mother is White and his father is mixed white and black, both his younger sisters who live with his grandmother look white, but for some reason, although Ermine looked white as well, he claims his father's one-half blackness.

"Jurist, Jurist, wait up!"

Ermine finally catches up with Jurist.

"What's up man? Why you walked out of history class yesterday? Mrs. Dandridge was about to write you up, but I told her your cousin had got killed in an accident and that you were having problems dealing with it."

"Man bump that cracker, I don't care about her writing me up."

"You better care and not do it anymore. The only way you're going to get to go to high school is to pass that cracker's class. All she asked you to do was not use the word nigger."

"Why I can't say the word nigga? White folks been calling us nigger since we got here they didn't have a problem with it then. But now all of a sudden we can't use it just because they can't use it anymore. The class didn't care about me using the word nigga in my paper. Man, bump her and bump school too. I know what the word nigga mean and so do the kids in that class room."

"For real man, what's wrong?" Ermine talked to Jurist in a smoother tone. "You're never going to be like your father and become a lawyer talking like that."

"We'll maybe I don't want to be like him anymore. Besides he died before he could make any money anyway. I'd rather be a construction worker like your step-dad at least he's still alive."

"Yeah barely, that nigga works three hours a day and drinks for the rest of the day. I wish he would leave or die one. Then I wouldn't have to worry about killing him the next time he hits my mama. But whatever's bothering you man you need to let it go and forget it. You want to go to Melrah to shoot some pool."

Ermine entices Jurist to come hang out with him, "All right," said Jurist, "I didn't want to go to school today anyway."

"I didn't say we weren't going to school. I just figured we'd get there a little late. Besides, I need to see if J.O. is there, he owes me some money from the last game we played."

"Why J.O owes you money?"

"We were playing a dollar a ball. I left that fool with four balls on the table."

Jurist finally cracks a smile and said, "That's still three more balls than you."

"I see we making jokes now."

"I wish I would have known that J.O owed you some money, I saw him make fifty dollars in no time when I was walking through the streets yesterday.

"For real. Now that's a job for you."

"What?"

"Serving! They make one, two and sometimes four-hundred dollars a day Jurist. Now that's some real money."

"Yeah, but what if you get caught. Then what?"
"Then, I'll just serve my time."

"Yeah, but that's some real time Ermine. Bump that, I'm not trying to go to jail. Besides that, my mama would kill me if she found out I was serving. Dog, you remember that time we saw Johnny and Tom smoking in the park and they said it was a cigarette. I saw Tom the other day and he said Johnny was getting out next week for having the rest of those cigarettes in the car with him when he got pulled over by the police."

"Damn he got 2 years. That's why I'll never get caught. I couldn't do that much time."

Ermine then looked at Jurist as they walk down the street, "Hey Jurist."

"What?"

"I'm glad you wrote that paper, bump that cracker we know what you meant."

Reassured of his friend's loyalty Jurist responds, "I know Ermine. That's why you my nigga."

Chapter 8
Company Man

TODAY IS JURIST'S FIRST DAY IN THE ELEVENTH GRADE and he's about to go to his last class for the day. The Eleventh grade is an important grade because it's the year of school where most students really start to think about life after high school and take steps to achieve their post-pubescent goals. Jurist does okay in school, but he has potential to do much better. Mr. Abdul Sharrieff, an educated, no nonsense brother from Philadelphia is Jurist's social studies teacher. Mr. Sharrieff is a former teacher from D.C that received his masters in History from an Ivy League College. Why he moved down here to Florida nobody really knows. In fact, no one in the community knows much of anything about him. The only thing anybody really knows is that he reads fanatically and does a lot of community service work.

"Good day students my name is Mr. Abdul Sharrieff. I am here to educate you on the behaviors of people and their civilizations or lack thereof. Moreover, I will teach you all that I know about the world, which isn't a lot, but it's still a little more than what you guys know. I am aware of the fact that you all have little to no knowledge about the social plights of cultures other than your own pervasive sub-cultures assuming that you have that much knowledge." Sitting at the back of the classroom is Jurist staring off in space thinking to himself. "There went my hopes of this being an easy class."

Walking from one side of the room to the other, Mr. Sharrieff gave his beginning of the year speech. "While you are in my class you will learn and even more important you will understand what you learn. Everyday people young and old shape and transform our surroundings and way of life. With each transformation an historic event occurs. I ask you to challenge yourself and decide how you will mark your place in history."

At the end of class everyone started packing their bags and putting away their books. Then the bell rang and the students began to walk out of the class. Mr. Sharrieff stopped Jurist. "Mr. Johnson, can I speak to you for a moment." Jurist walked over to Mr. Sharrieff in a reserved manner. You're Pharaoh's son aren't you?

"Yeah. Why? Did you know my father?" Jurist replied.

"No, but I have been told many great things about him. I heard he was a really, good man. I hope you're striving to be even greater."

"I'm not trying to be no different than you or any other man."

"How are you doing at this school?"

"I'm doing."

"Are you involved in any after-school activities?"

"Nall, I've never been too interested in playing organized sports."

"What about academic activities such as the Brain Bowl, I'm in charge of the History Brain Bowl team. Tryouts are next week. You should come and try to make the team."

"No thanks, I'm to busy."

"You sure, the schools are giving a $500.00 scholarship to the winners of each district." "You do plan to go to college, don't you?" In a contained and mildly aggressive voice Jurist responded, "I don't know."

"Jurist, I want you to understand something if you don't remember anything else I teach you. There are several systems that encompass every aspect of our lives. So if you ever want to truly triumph over the system that you believe is defeating you, you must first learn how that system works."

"Yeah man, whatever," Jurist clandestinely replies.

Jurist leaves the classroom and walk down the hall to meet up with Ermine near their lockers. "Damn man what took you so long?" Ermine asked Jurist.

While Ermine and Jurist are talking, some guys across from them are making comments about Shayla. Shayla is a pretty, natural looking young lady with mocha skin and soulful eyes not to mention a very keen mind and sharp tongue. One of the young brothers tried a flawed attempt to get her attention.

"Piss, piss hey girl, I know you hear me." The other boy to scared to even try to talk to her himself, boost the other young man to touch Shayla. "I bet you won't touch her booty." But neither of them was aware that Shayla had heard their little plot and she was hell bent on making sure the little bet of theirs wouldn't have a chance to manifest. Shayla walked over to the locker of the boys and with fire in her eyes she said, "I bet he won't either." Her eyes looked as ferocious as a lioness on the plains of Africa. And that was all they heard before she walked away and deafeningly slammed her locker door.

Ermine and Jurist stood there in awe of the sisters domineering status and stature. Ermine whispered to Jurist, "Damn boy that girl fine as hell, but she's just too mean."

"Yeah, I think she might be dating one of those football niggas." Jurist told Ermine the little information that he thinks he knows about her.

"Man, I bet they be running trains on her all the time."

"I don't know man, she goes to the same church my mama goes to."

"What's that suppose to mean? Ermine stopped leaning on the locker and took a more upright position. "Those be the freaky ones. She's not that fine for nothing. Somebody's getting it."

"Well we both know who's not."

"Yeah, you!" Jurist and Ermine both shout out in unison.

Then they start laughing. A couple seconds pass by and Ermine greets Jurist with a challenge, "I bet I get her before you do."

"You think so."

"Hell yeah! You know how the ladies just love us high yellow niggas."

"Nigga, you ain't yellow, you White. But if you think you can, go get her then."

"Come on, let's see where she's going."

They follow her around the corner of the gym.

"Looked like she going to the cafeteria. Jurist, what they got going on in there."

"That's where they're having that stupid History Brain Bowl tryout."

"Man, you all into that history shit. Why don't you tryout?"

"That's for them nerdy ass niggas that want to show off how smart they think they are."

"Well that fits you to a exactly, besides if all the girls in there are as fine as Shayla then I'm about to become a nerd."

While the boys are talking and looking through the window Mr. Sharrieff walked up behind them; startling them both with his presence. "Are you young men just going to stand out here and peep or are you all going to come in so you can hear as well.

"Damn, man you scared the hell out of me." A stunned Ermine replied.

"Look, something good has come about all ready." Mr. Sharrieff responded, referring to Ermine saying hell was scared out of him.

"No, we're not coming in. We were just looking." Jurist tried to reassure Mr. Sharrieff that he has no intentions of joining his after school brain bowl team.

"What you afraid you might find out you don't know as much as you think you know."

Offended by Mr. Sharrieff's remark and confident in Jurist's capability and knowledge of history, Ermine reciprocated with, "Man you must be crazy. I bet my dog knows more than any of those fools in there."

"How much!" Replied Mr. Sharrieff.

"Jurist, you hear him. What's up dog, you ready to make some money?"

"Always!" Jurist hesitantly answer back.

"Twenty-dollars! Ten for Jurist and ten for me."

"Bet. But if I win you must stop calling each other dogs and niggas and Jurist you have to join the team."

"Bet," Jurist responds as he looked straight into Mr. Sharrieff delving eyes, then he glanced over at his main man Ermine, who he knew had complete confidence in him. If Ermine wasn't there Jurist would have certainly turned down such a bet. But when Ermine has his back there is no challenge Jurist feels is too great. So they all walk into the cafeteria. There were about three groups of fours and one group of three people totaling the fifteen people who came to tryout who were fiercely in conversation and debate with one another. That is until Mr. Sharrieff walked through the door with Ermine and Jurist. Most of the kids trying out were on the team the previous year and they weren't expecting any new comers especially not the likes of those two.

"Shayla, can you please come here." Mr. Sharrieff asked.

Shayla rushed over from her group of skilled peers wondering what Mr. Sharieff could possibly want to talk to her about with Jurist and Ermine there. "This is Jurist; he's going to be your first challenger this season." This was a situation that Jurist was not prepared for. He was more than willing to go inside the cafeteria and make silly, boyish remarks, but Shayla was a little intimidating plus she was a girl. "Hold up, you didn't say her. I thought you were talking about one of those guys." Jurist responded in a timid voice.

"What, are you scared you're going to get beat by a girl? Shayla, smirks and taunts Jurist. "Well don't be! Because I'm a lady, I'll take it easy on you. This being your first time and all." The girls in the cafeteria start to laugh. Then one of the girls from the group that she left yelled. "Yeah girl, take it easy on the virgin." Shayla and the other girls remarks chopped at Jurist's masculine pride like an axe to wood but Jurist wasn't about to fall over with one swing. So he looked her in the eyes and said, "I just didn't want to embarrass you. A grown man like myself taking advantage of a poor little naive girl, that's not fair."

"Just don't embarrass yourself and fall short of the answer. Why don't you just quit now while you still have a chance to leave with whatever self-esteem you still have intact."

Before this match of slick comments and innuendoes went any further Mr. Sharrieff stepped in, "Hey, hey, hey ya'll calm down. Here are the rules. Each of you are going to have one attempt at answering 10 questions; you will receive one point for each correct answer, and two points for answering a question that the other person responds to incorrectly. The person with the most points at the end wins. Now, ya'll follow me, except for you Ermine you can stay here on the floor."

With the eyes of everyone in the cafeteria on them, they all walked up the steps to the stage towards the back of the cafeteria. On the stage there stood two podiums about ten feet apart.

"Shayla you get on my left and Jurist you stand at the podium to my right." Then Mr. Sharrieff walked to the table in the center of them both, sat down in the chair and picked up the microphone that was on the table. "All right everyone I have a treat for you today, Jurist here to my right is challenging Shayla for a spot on the team. Mr. Sharrieff looked over to Shayla, then he looked over at Jurist, "Jurist you all have 5 seconds to answer the question given to you and we are going to start with you first. Who was the first African American to earn a doctorate degree here in the US?"

Jurist answered the question swiftly, "W.E.B. Dubois."

"Correct. Shayla! Who is considered to be the father of Black History?"

"Carter G. Woodson," she answered a half-second after he asked the question.

After seven straight correct answers from them both, it's on Jurist to answer this next question. Neither of them has taken more than three seconds to answer any of the questions. The crowd has gotten

45

up from their seats and joined Ermine at the front of the stage. There are whispers amongst those voicing on who they think will win. This is a far different attitude than they had when Jurist and Shayla's challenge was first announced. They were all sure that Shayla the two-time District Champion would easily roll over the newcomer. But the battle of knowledge continues.

"Jurist, who was responsible for the first successful Black slave revolution in Haiti?"

"Easy, Toussaint L 'Ouverture"

"Correct. Shayla, he was born a slave in Maryland and developed his speaking skills in a secret debating club?"
"Fredrick Douglas"

"Jurist, what was the name of the club?"

"The East Baltimore Mental Improvement Society"

"Correct"

Ermine screamed from the sideline, "Only one more to go and we win man."

Mr. Sharrieff stared coldly at Ermine not only because he is interrupting the match but also because of his usage of the word man.

"Shayla, what was the name of the man charged in the 1964 Alabama Church bombing?"

"No one was ever charged."

"Correct"

"Jurist, what is the ancient name of Egypt?"

"I pass."

Ermine shocked by Jurist's answer, yells out, "You what!" Even the crowd is in disbelief. The two had been moving like a well oiled engine for eighteen straight correct answers. The crowd had started to believe that neither of them would ever get one wrong. "Shayla, do you know the answer?"

With no hesitation she answered, "Kemet!"

"That's correct. Shayla wins ten to nine."
Ermine disgusted with the outcome, damn man we lost. Then he looked at Mr. Sharrieff and smiled and said, "I had to get one in for old-time's sake."

In the meantime, Jurist quietly walked over to Shayla.

 "Congratulation Shayla, you are almost as smart as you think you are." He then extends his hand out to her.

"Thanks. You're not that dumb yourself. Have you competed before?"

"No, I just like to read sometimes."

Mr. Sharrieff and Ermine walked up to them both. "So, I'll see you at practice tomorrow Jurist."

But before Jurist could answer Ermine intervened and answered from him. "Yeah, you'll see him. Come on Jurist, let's bail." While he walked out with Ermine he looked back at Shayla and said.

"I guess I'll see ya'll tomorrow at practice."

While Jurist and Ermine are walking home all they can talk about was Shayla and the game.

"Man, this is your chance."

"Chance for what?" Jurist answered back puzzled.

"Dah stupid, to get with Shayla. Man, she was digging you."

"Yeah, you think. For real, stop playing."

"Man, I was watching her eyes. She couldn't take them off you.
Man, you got her. That was brilliant how you let her win in the end.
Women love when they think they can beat their man at something.
Especially, if they feel they can't."

Chapter 9
Glistening Flower

THREE WEEKS HAVE PAST BY and Jurist and Shayla have built a nice rapport with one another. Although it seems as if they put one another down a lot, their relationship can almost be characterized with the play of leopard cubs. Nonetheless, today is the only day that they have ever been left alone with one another. Shayla is collecting all the practice material and Jurist is picking up trash off the floor. After talking to one of the other team members

Mr. Sharrieff steps back into the practice room. "Shayla do you need a ride home?" He asked.

"No I'm okay. Jurist said he would walk me home."

Jurist turned around and looked at her with a surprise stare because he didn't remember telling Shayla that he would walk her home today.

"All right, I'll see you all at practice tomorrow."
Mr. Sharrieff leaves the room.

"When did I volunteer to walk you home?"
"What, you don't want to?"

"I didn't say that."

"Well what are you saying?"

"I guess I'm saying yeah."

"I thought so." Shalya confidently walked closer to Jurist. "It ain't like that now."

"Well we'll see how it is."

"Aren't you dating one of the football players?"

"To be so intelligent, you sure do ask a lot of brainless questions."

"How is that a dumb question?"

"Because you're assuming something you have no reason to assume. Besides if I had a boyfriend do you think I would have asked you to walk me home."

"I don't know; you might be that type of girl."

"Well trust me I'm not like any girl you know. So tell me something Jurist."

"What?"

"What's the deepest thought you have that you don't share with anyone?"

"Why should I tell you?"

"Because if you tell me, and I believe you, I'll tell you mine?"

"I guess I just want to know why we are here." Shayla became very intrigued with Jurist answer and felt as if she had to know more.

"Can you elaborate please?"

"Why are we here? Why out of everybody in the world did they choose my people to be their slaves and why didn't God protect my daddy?"

"When you say they; to whom are you referring to?"

"What you mean who I'm referring to? White people! Who you think I'm talking about?" Jurist spoke in a more stern fashion. In a sincere voice of concern Shayla answered back, "You really hate white people don't you?" Jurist turned away from Shayla while taking a deep breath as if he was about to take a dive into a pool of exclusive thoughts. But Shayla, intent on being welcomed into Jurist most intimate thoughts grabbed his hand to let him know that he is not alone. "Hate is a strong emotion that only clouds your thoughts and obscures your judgment." Shayla stopped walking and looked Jurist directly in his eyes. "It's safe to hate if you choose not to challenge your adversary, but if you ever decide to challenge anyone or thing including white people you must first learn to free yourself from your hate. Hate is a petty weakness that can be easily exploited."

"How can you not hate them? When you know that they're the ones responsible for us living in this backwards world. Did they not hate us? We abide by their laws, we learn their culture, and we succumb to their ideas about how we should look and how we should live our lives. Somebody's responsible for the way we live. Look at their neighborhoods and look at ours. And you have the nerve to tell me that I can't hate them."

"Hold up Jurist, that didn't sound like hate to me. In fact, it sounds more like envy. The only person that can determine how you live is you. Okay grant it, Black people have it hard here in America. So what people have it bad everywhere! You just have to find your purpose for being. Freedom comes through knowledge and prosperity is a result of progress not hate and we as a people will never progress until we rid ourselves of hate both outward and inward."

"Oh yeah, well tell that to the thousands of people who were mutilated, raped, hung, and burned. Tell that to the generations of children who are fatherless because of the White man's hate. I mean you talk as if you don't care about what they did, what they're doing and what they're going to do to our people. So what's your purpose?" Jurist asked Shayla with a fire in his heart.

"To make sure you and others like yourself become the men you are supposed to become," Shayla responds as only a woman could. They stare into each other's eyes timelessly without a word being spoken until Jurist breaks the tension.

"What's up with you thinking you know the answers to everything?" Shayla gave a half smile, "If I can recall correctly, Eve was the first to eat from the Tree of Knowledge. Adam only got to eat what was left over."

They both smile and laugh.

"That's my house there." Shayla points to the blue, white and brick house.

"Nice house."

"Thanks, but it actually belongs to my step-dad. He's cool. He wants to marry my mom, but she wants to see how he acts with us staying here before she accepts his proposal."

"Now I see where you get your meticulous foresight."

"So, we're using big words now."

"I'm sorry I didn't know meticulous was a big word to you." Shayla smiled at Jurist as if her soul was filled with the purest of happiness.

"Your smile."

"What about it?"

"It's like a glistening flower. Every time I see it, it reminds me of how even the most tumultuous storm can help to make beauty even more beautiful. Why haven't I ever seen this side of you before?"

"Maybe you were too scared to get to know me."

"Maybe," Jurist affectionately answered back.

"Thanks for walking me home Jurist."

"Any time!"

"Is that a promise?"

"Of course," Jurist responds while backing away from Shayla's driveway, "You're my glistening flower."

Shayla continues to look at Jurist from her yard in a way that made him develop feelings that only a girl can make a boy feel.

Chapter 10
Brain Bowl

A COUPLE OF WEEKS HAVE PASSED BY and Jurist has quickly become a rising star and fierce competitor within the Brain Bowl arena. Jurist and Shayla share ten first-place and six second place finishes. As a team they are ranked number one in their region. The entire county believes that it is a good chance that they will have to compete against one another in the finals for individual champion. This would be a historical event. Especially when you take into account that only once in the past ten years has two individuals from the same team had to encounter one another in the finals. The team has just finished practice for today and Mr. Sharrieff is about to tell everyone the results of the final Brain Bowl selection team.

"All right team, the Brain Bowl championship is next week. We have four people who qualified. I know that you all don't want to wait any longer to know so here they are. Chad, Shayla, Jurist and Sean congratulations, one of you will have the opportunity to win a $500 scholarship. To everyone that didn't qualify individually I don't want you all to get to down in the dumps because we still have an opportunity to win as a team. I'm proud of all of you. Now can I get a big Go Eagles!

"Go Eagles" They all shouted.

"Shayla may I talk with you for a second please."

Shayla walked over to Mr. Sharrieff, Jurist turned his head and watches with curiosity. Mr. Sharrieff gave Shayla a big smile and words of endearment. Then Shayla walked back over to Jurist. "Shayla I must admit that I have been watching you and Mr. Sharrieff and sometimes ya'll talk to each other in a weird way. Well not really weird but weird for a teacher and student. Ya'll seem to have a loving type of affection for one another. How long have you two known each other? With paramount attention Jurist waits for an answer.

Shayla responds, "I've known him all my life."

"Oh yeah, is he a friend of your family or something?"

"I guess you can say that. Jurist, can you keep a secret?" Shayla asked, as she gently grabbed Jurist's bicep and directs him away from everyone.

"Yes, of course I can."

Shayla's hand slips down to Jurist's wrist "Follow me." Shayla and Jurist walked out of the cafeteria where the practice is being held.

"Jurist, what I'm about to tell you I don't want you to tell anybody. Understand."

"Yeah I understand."

"Jurist, Mr. Sharrieff is my brother."

"Woe, that's a relief," Jurist gasps, as he grins.

"What? Why, you smiling?" Shayla asked.

"Because, I thought you were about to say you all were fooling around or something."

"Boy, you so silly!"

"Why don't ya'll want anybody to know?"

"It's not really anyone else's business. And I would appreciate it if nobody found out."

"Shayla can I be honest with you?"

"I should hope so. Why have you been lying to me?"

"Of course not, I mean I have something to tell you."

"What?"

Just as Shayla is finishing her comment Jurist leaned over and kisses her. A minute later she said, "I thought you were going to tell me something."

"I want you to be my girlfriend.

"Boy, is that all. I've known that. What you just figured that out?" I became your girlfriend the first day you walked me home.

They both smile then Jurist grabbed Shayla and hugs her tightly as he started spinning her around.

Laughing and smiling, Shayla playfully told Jurist to stop. "Stop, Jurist, stop, you're going to make me dizzy."

They smile at each other and kiss again.

"Come on boy and walk me home it's starting to get late. The street lights are about to come on. I saw my mom season a couple of hen maybe you can stay for dinner."

"That would be great; I just have to call my mama when I get to your house."

After dinner Shayla and Jurist go outside to her front yard.

Nightfall has come and the stars are shining bright and a shooting star just danced across the sky directly above Shayla and Jurist as they sit under the tree.

"Jurist what are your aspirations?"

"What do you mean?"

"I mean what do you what to do with the rest of your life?"
"Saying it is easy. Support my mom, rear a family. You know have the American Dream."

"Where; here in the United States? Is the US the only place you want to live?"

"America is the only place I know."

"Yeah, but you live in the United States."

"What's the difference?"

"One is a place and the other is an idea."

"What's up with you and your brother, Shayla stared hard at Jurist to reminding him of his promise to keep her and Mr. Sharrieff's relationship a secret. I mean Mr. Sharrieff? Both of you always come at me with these deep, philosophical questions."

Realizing that she maybe insulting Jurist ability to be discreet about her and Mr. Sharrieff's relationship she responds, "My brother told me that we must use our knowledge plus our third eye to define life. Moreover, he teaches me to look at the world around me not for what it appears to be, but for what it actually is through the forethought of our soul."

"I wish I could learn to look at the world the way you look at it." Jurist responds.

"You can and many other ways as well, I'm sure he'll be happy to help you open your third eye."

"I don't know Shayla. What, I'm supposed to go to him and be like hey Mr. Sharrieff can you open my third eye for me."

Shayla smiled, "No silly, just ask him to teach you as he would teach himself if he was you. After all you are his number one guy."

Chapter 11
Thug Life

IT'S THE SECOND NINE WEEKS OF SENIOR YEAR, Jurist and Ermine haven't seen a lot of one another but they're still great friends. However, Ermine isn't going to school as much. In truth, he has been spending most his time in the streets and pool rooms gambling and selling marijuana. The streets are always packed with traffic and Ermine has fit in like a brand new mustang blending into the scenery of a car show. On every corner there is somebody hustling something and the police are almost nonexistent.

Frequently, you see crack heads and prostitutes hounding the drug dealers for deals and favors. But for the most part everything is at deadly peace. On the corner of South Bee Avenue and 16th street is Melrah that's where Ermine is at religiously on every Friday.

Different people may give different reasons but the truth of the matter is, that's when all the local gamblers and hustlers are all out doing their thing. People have gotten paid and looking to relax and have a good time. But for Ermine and the rest of the hustlers it's the beginning of his work week. Ermine might not leave the block until Monday morning because everyone who lives a street life has at least dual employment. Yeah, he's cool with the guys he shares a block with but as the saying goes keep your friends close and your enemies closer. If you are as good as gambler as you are hustler you can quadruple the money you get from selling dope by shooting craps or playing cards. Hell, on the corner you can make money pitching pennies. Any way they can get it, a true hustler will. The mission statement of every street is get money. There is no real love on the streets; the true nature of capitalism prevents it. How could it be? Most of the people on the streets hustling came from homes void of friendly compassion. The streets are business and business is the streets. But in reality every street business is a gamble and a hustle even Wall Street.

"Come on Li Joe!" Ermine shouted out.

Then a few seconds later somebody yells, "Here comes them boys." Everyone looked over his or her shoulder because that usually means that the police are somewhere near.

Jimmy is a fairly large brother that likes to shine especially when it came to gold. Jimmy has twelve gold teeth six at the top, six at the bottom and he keeps a gold chain and medallion of Christ around his neck. "Hold dice, Hold dice." He exclaims because he thinks that the presents of the police is a good enough reason to stop play. J.O however, a light-skinned brother from Detroit has a different opinion. "Man, fuck the police. They aren't about to bother us."

Ermine then tried to bring the attention back to the crap game.

"What ya'll need to worry about is this deuce, deuce I'm about to roll." That's when Deion, a young dropout from the Breeze projects, steps over to the game to talk to Ermine. "E, hey E, you straight?" Ermine responds with frustration in his voice. "Hold up man, don't you see me shooting nigga." Meanwhile, one of the dice has stop spinning and has landed on two while the second dice continue to spin. Ermine then tried to cheer the other dice on to do the same as the first dice. "Come on deuce, come on."

J.O came back with, "I know this nigga about to go out now. This nigga begging the dice and everything."

60

Jimmy stoops quietly as he enthusiastically asked for the other dice to land on a five. "Kick him in his ass 5."

J.O then tried to increase the wager to twenty dollars. Ermine quickly accepts the bet. Soon after the other dice stopped and a five appears and everybody picked up their money.

Ermine instinctively turned to his left and looked at Deion three times more ferociously abusive stare of his stepfather.

"Damn, nigga. You round here bothering a nigga, giving me all that bad ass luck. What you want?"

Deion then request that Ermine sell him a nickel bag of marijuana. This request infuriates Ermine, "Nigga you fucking with me while I'm shooting for a damn nic. He'll nall, I ain't got no damn nics. As a matter of fact don't you ever ask me for anything again. You stupid mother."

Then right before Ermine is about to burst from anger Jurist walked up and sobers him.

"E, E let me holla at you."

"You better be glad my nigga called me, Ermine said as he walked away from the crap game. What's up Chief? Hey fellas I'll be back in a minute. Deion, don't look or say anything to me ever again or else I'm going to remember this moment. What's up J, What you been up to J?"

"Just trying to finish this school thing, that's all."

"Where's your girl? Usually I can't see you without seeing her."

"I think she's over to one of her girls crib."

"Tell her I said she needs to hook me up with one of those smart ass friends of hers."

"All right, I'll tell her. You went to school today."

"Nall man, I couldn't make it today. Today's Friday, payday and the first of the month."

Ermine then put one of his hands in his pocket. "You need a little change."

"No, I'm cool. I appreciate it though. I just wanted to see how you did on the ACT."

"Man, I walked out before I finished. Man, I wasn't wit that shit. I couldn't take being in that room all that time just taking a test."

"So, what you gonna do about college."

"I don't even know if I'm going or not."

"Cuz, you can't keep doing this all your life."

"I know, but college ain't for me cuz."

"How about we talk about this tonight at my house, my mama's cooking some chicken, greens, macaroni and cornbread tonight. You should come by?"

"Hell, yeah! What time Mrs. J going to be finish cooking?"

"Around seven or eight."

"I'll be there at seven."

"All right man you be safe now."

"Bruh, you know me, I'm safer than that condom your daddy was wearing. They chuckle and give each other dap.

Then Jurist leaves and Ermines walked back over to finish is dice game.

"All right fellas, who's rolling?"

When Jurist makes it home he saw his mother in the kitchen.
"Good evening, Ma."

"Good evening, Jurist."

"Ma, make sure you make enough for Ermine. He said he was going to come by."

"That's good; I want to talk to that boy. He's been up on that corner a little too often."

"Ma, don't harass and irritate the boy when he gets here."

"I'm not going to irritate nobody. I just want to ask him about his plans for the future. You all will be graduating soon. By the way, have you and that girlfriend of yours decided where you're going to apply."

"Not yet, but Mr. Sharrieff said he has a couple of connections at some really good colleges."

"Just make sure whatever you decide to do it's your decision."
"What's that suppose to mean."

"I mean you have control over your life. Live your life and make decisions in your life that's going to make you happy. Don't get me wrong. Mr. Sharrieff is a good man and I appreciate the extra time he spends helping you become a better student. But I just want you to remember that you have the right to make your own decisions even if Mr. Sharrieff don't agree with them. OK!"

"Ok, ma."

"I love you baby."

"I love you to Ma."

Meanwhile, on the other side of town, Ermine's stepfather John Putnam has just walked in the house from a half days work. Drunk as usual, with a bad attitude, he stumbles through the front door yelling. "Eve, Eve where is my money?"

Eve rushed to the door in a wifely manner. "What money John?"

"The money I had in my wallet."

Nervously timid she responds, "Oh I had to take a hundred dollars yesterday to pay the light bill."

In a slow slurred voice he asked her, "Why didn't you ask me for it?"

"John, you were sleep and you wouldn't get up and if I didn't pay it by noon they were going to turn off the electricity."

John drunk and filled with anger soon became infuriated and grabbed Eve by her hair.

"Listen here you little cunt, don't you ever go in my wallet. You hear me? I took off half the day because I thought that I had lost my money."

"I'm sorry John but I had to take it, they were going to cut off the lights."

"You no good liar the lights are on."

John slaps Eve and Eve started to cry. "Shut up, stop that damn crying I barely touched you. Shut up I said." Before she knew it John slapped her so hard she fell straight to the floor.

"John please, please John stop. The lights are on because I already paid the bill."

"No you stop. Stop your lying bitch! Where's my money?"

John began striking her repeatedly, ever blow harder than before. Battered and crying, Eve continues to plea for mercy, "John I swear to you I paid the light bill with it."

But no matter how hard Eve cried John only hit her harder and harder until he couldn't hear her cry any longer.

J.O a gambling buddy of Ermine lives in the same building and walked by the open door and saw the brutal beaten that John was putting on Eve and called an ambulance for her. And since he and Ermine hung on the corner together he knew exactly where Ermine would be so he left to go ride by the corner to tell Ermine the bad news.

Riding in his brand new lower rider truck J.O spots Ermine on the corner near Melrah shooting craps. So he hollered at him from the truck.

"E, E" J.O screamed, "Come here."

"What, don't you see a nigga busy?"

"This is important the ambulance just took your mama to the hospital."

"What," Ermine jumped up from the crap game. "Dog you'll give me a ride up there?"

"Yeah, come on."

Ermine and J.O arrived at the hospital in mere minutes.

"J.O thanks man I appreciate the ride."

"No problem man, I just hope she's all right."

Ermine rushed up to the hospital's receptionist desk. "I'm looking for Eve Putnam's room."

The receptionist responds, "Hold on one minute. Let me check the computer to see if we have her in a room already. She might still be in the emergency room."

"You have to have her here she just came in on the ambulance."

"Yes, we do have her. She's still in the ER. What's your name sir?"

"I'm her son Ermine."

"Go over to those doors and I'll buzz you in. She's the third room on the right."

Ermine sprints through the doors and to his mother's room. His breathing rate is at least twice the normal speed as he dashes in her room and asked, "Mama, what happened?"

Eve barely conscious responds, "He got mad at me because I told him I took his money out of his pants to pay the light bill."

Ermine became enraged with anger. "He did what?"

Eve saw Ermine's face rapidly change from one of worrisome to festering hostility.

"Ermine don't be mad he was right. I had no business going into his pants pocket without him knowing."

But Eve's words feel upon death ears because Ermine is paying no attention to what she just said. All he can see is her ruthlessly beaten face and imagine the pain and agony she must be baring. His eyes motionless with disgust, stared at the way his mother's mouth unnaturally moves because of her swollen jaw.

Then Ermine vaguely mumbles, "I'm going to kill that nigga."
Eve fearful of actions that her son may take pleads with Ermine,
"Baby, don't do nothing crazy."

As tears run down Ermine's face he verbalize his thoughts, "Ma, he
ain't got no right to hurt you like this."

A tear ran down Ermine's cheek. Eve reached up to wash away
Ermine's tears. Ermine then glanced over Eve's entire body, and he
noticed how her arms have bruises on them that look as if she had
been kicked and punched over like a gym bag.

"Baby, don't worry about it." Eve collected whatever strength she
has to beg her son to subjugate his antagonistic feelings, "I'm ok.
He's just going through a lot right now."

But this pleading only made the hate within Ermine boil even
hotter.

"He ain't gone through nothing yet."

Ermine rushed out of the hospital room with thoughts of vengeance
echoing through his syntax.

"No Ermine let him be, come back Ermine, come back," she
screamed.

Ermine ran out of the hospital in a stallion's stride. He didn't have
a clue as to what he was going to do until he had ran half way home.
That's when he really stopped to think about what he was going to
do. So he devised a scheme and all he needed was a gun and a
partner. Therefore, he ran to the only place he knew he could get a
gun and fast. After that he ran to Jurist house.

Ermine knocked on Jurist's door only twice before Jurist opened it.
Before Ermine could say a word Jurist noticed that something was
terribly wrong, "What's up with you cuz?" Jurist questioned him

lightly.

"I'm gonna kill that nigga."

"Who?"

"My good for nothing step-daddy. He beat my mama up bad this time man. She's in the hospital right now! But a hospital isn't going to be able to help him once I'm through with him." Suddenly and without notice Ermine lifts up his shirt and shows Jurist the gun that he had just brought.

"Hold up E. Where did you get that from?"

"I got it from Dee before I came over here."

"You need to think about this first."

"Think, I can't stop thinking; I'm tired of thinking."

"Dog, he's not worth it. Don't trade your life for his."

"Fuck that! Suppose it was your mama. What would you do?"

"I don't know, but I know I would want you to do the same thing I'm trying to do. E, listen to reason, I know you're mad and hurt right now but believe me what you're thinking isn't going to make anything better."

Ermine agitated by Jurist remarks and hesitation to come with him he then gave Jurist an ultimatum, "Man, I'm tired of all this talking you coming or what?"

"I'm not going and neither are you E. I'm sorry man but I can't let you go over there like this."

That's when Ermine lifts his gun up and points it at Jurist. "I'm sorry cuz but I don't see how you can stop me."

Jurist mom Nandi hears the boys talking outside and started to make her way towards the door.

"Jurist, what's going on out there? Is that Ermine at the door, ya'll need to come in to eat and close the door before the mosquitoes get in here."

"E, if you do this they will give you life."

"Only if they catch me or you tell."

Then as rapidly as he came, Ermine tucks away his gun and took off running down the road. Soon after, Nandi walked up behind Jurist, "Jurist what's going on, what's wrong, why is Ermine running down the road?"

In an emotionlessly, shocked demeanor Jurist answered his mother, "His step-dad beat up his mother again and he said that he's going to kill him."

"Damn, that poor boy. You couldn't talk him out of it?

"I tried to but he was so mad that he wasn't trying to hear what I had to say."

"Jurist, I know Ermine is your friend and all but whatever's going on with Ermine and his family that's something him and his family has to deal with themselves."

"But ma he's my best friend."

"And you're my only son and I'm not letting you endanger your life by getting involved with this any further. The best thing you can do for Ermine now is pray. We can go to your room and I'll pray with you if you want me to, unless you want to talk about it some more.

"All right ma I'm going to my room, but I don't think I'm going to feel like eating any time soon."

"I understand, I'll fix you a plate and put it up for you."

Nandi gave Jurist a long affectionate hug and kiss on his forehead. Meanwhile, Ermine is still running to his house to find his stepfather. As Jurist laid down on his bed, he began to contemplate about his friendship with Ermine and all the things they had done for one another. Eventually, he fall asleep and has a dream about Ermine and his stepfather. In his dream, the room is pitch-black with hatred swimming around the room like piranhas. Ermine's stepfather came home to his apartment and tried to turn on the lamp by the door but it doesn't work. So he began to feel his way to his room but as soon as he entered the room Ermine struck him with a massive blow to his head. When he falls to his knees, Ermine kicks him in the stomach then on his back. After he finishes kicking and punching Mr. Putnam, he rolled him over on his back and said "I'll see you in hell" and shoots him three times in the chest area. Jurist immediately wakes up breathing very rapidly and looking in every direction. Jurist then rolled out of his bed, put on his shoes and climbed through his window.

Chapter 12
Faith of a Friend

It's early Saturday morning and Nandi is listening to the local
gospel station on the radio as she does every Saturday before she
prepares breakfast for Jurist and herself. All over the house you
hear a young, strong voice with the soulful sound of an evangelist,
"Speak Lord, speak to me, speak my Lord, speak to me, I'm so
tired," then all of a sudden the song is interrupted by a special news
report.

"Hi I'm Jim Loveless, pardon the interruption of your usually
scheduled show, but we have some late breaking news. This
morning at 3:55 a.m., a white male named John Putnam was found
murdered in his apartment. Neighbors stated that they heard
shooting in the Round Tower apartment complex and decided to
call to inform the police. They later told police that they originally
thought that he had probably committed suicide. It is alleged that
yesterday Mr. Putnam came home drunk and beat his wife so badly
that she had to be rushed to a hospital. The shooter's identity has
not yet been determined and police officials say that although they
don't have a suspect in custody, they do have a lead but are unable
to release any names. If you have any information regarding this
crime, please contact your local law enforcement agency. Then just
like nothing happened the music picked back up in progress. "May

be god is trying to tell you something," But the music is soon over shadowed by the commanding sound of Nandi as she instantly called for Jurist. "Jurist, Jurist wake up and come here, baby."

With cold in his eyes and mouth wide open as he yawns, Jurist walked out of his room wearing only his boxers, and a T-shirt as he totter towards the kitchen.

Getting straight to the point Nandi said to Jurist, "I think Ermine killed his step-daddy last night. Nandi turned and grabbed Jurist by his shoulders. You need to stay as far away from that boy as possible. I know he's your friend and all, but the police are already on the lookout. They even interrupted the gospel show on the radio this morning that's why I woke you up a little bit earlier."

Jurist with a distilled look on his face answered her, "Don't worry ma, I won't see him, he's gone. Ain't nobody going to see him for a while."

Later on that afternoon Mr. Sharrieff and Shayla are sitting in the kitchen at Mr. Sharrieff's house talking.

"So Shay, how are you and Jurist getting along? Because it seems to me that things have gotten very serious between you two. I knew something was happening between you two after he let you win that first challenge I put you all up to."

"Whatever, he did not let me win anything, he just froze."

"Yeah but the only time he ever freezes is when he has you as an adversary."

"So what you think he's a better player than me."

"I'm not saying all that. Although his first year record is better than yours. I'm just saying that you like to win and he likes to see you win no matter what the cost is to him personally."

"Yeah, yeah, yeah, anyways, Jurist knows who the better player is, but to answer your question. Yes, we're doing fine, why?"

"That's cool, I'm glad to see my little sister start to take interest in someone and Jurist is a good boy and he's going to grow to be a fine man. So, you really like him, ha?"

"Yeah you can say that."

"Do you think you love him?

"I don't know. Why you asking me all these questions? You're acting too much like mama right now. I all ready have to hear her mouth," Shayla began to imitate her mother; "You really like Jurist. Ya'll make such a cute couple. The next time you invite Jurist over, can you tell Jurist that I need him to help me with the yard."

Mr. Sharrieff interrupts with another question. "How you think he feels about you?" Mr. Sharrieff digs deeper into what Shayla thinks about her and Jurist relationship.

"I think he feels the same."

"Guess what."

"What"

"I have a surprise for the both of you."

"Well, what is it?"

"I got you both accepted into the State of Florida University, with I might add, four year scholarships."

"Abdul are you serious? Shayla is ecstatic with the news of her and Jurist receiving scholarships. "Abdul, that's great. I can kiss you right now. Jurist is going to be so happy to hear this. Since Ermine left, he has been really down and irritable. He needs some good news right now."

"Why don't you invite him over for dinner tonight? You can cook and we'll celebrate."

"Ok! But first I have something to tell you."

"What is it?"

"I told Jurist about us being family. You're not mad are you?"

"No, I'm not mad I figured you had. It's ok. Jurist is one of the family."

"I love you big Bruh."

"I love you too. Lil sis."

Shayla gave Mr. Sharrieff a kiss on the cheek, grabbed her purse off the couch and walked out the door to go see Jurist. In the meantime, Mr. Sharrieff goes back to his office and sat at his desk. He looked around his room at the pictures on the walls, which are all prominent African-American and African men from different periods of time. He began to stare at this one particular design that looked like it had been personally designed and closed his eyes. After he opened his eyes he reached in his bottom desk draw and picked up a cell phone. The phone rang twice and a young lady picked up the phone.

"Yes, this is Abdul Sharrieff I need to speak to Professor Conan, please."

"Hold please."

She buzzes Professor Conan's office.

"Mr. Abdul Sharrieff on line 4."

"I'll take it. Sharrieff, how are we doing today?"

"We are fine. She's on her way to tell him now. I'm going to send them both up to meet with you next week."

"I hope we're making the right choice" said Professor Conan with a little doubtfulness in his voice.

"Trust me, he's perfect."

"He better be, we've invested a lot of time into this project of yours."

"I'll call you back later tonight after we have dinner to celebrate your gracious gift. Progress through Knowledge..."

"Prosperity through Freedom," Professor Conan finishes the phrase.

Chapter 13
The Opportunity

BEFORE SHAYLA KNOCKED ON THE JOHNSON'S FRONT DOOR, she noticed two black boys getting into a car. Each boy had a quart of beer in his hands and she could tell by the way that they were walking that it wasn't the first one they had gotten a hold of today. She then over heard the boys' conversation as they talk about staying drunk all day before they go to the club tonight.

As they are getting in the car two kids riding a big wheel slowly approaches the rear of the vehicle. The boys too caught up in their own conversation to notice the children and are totally unaware of their position. As soon as they get ready to back up Shayla screamed out to the driver, "Hey watch out for the kids!"

The boy surprised that Shayla is even talking to him stopped what he was doing and looked over at Shayla. "What!" Shayla completely pissed off at the boys' irresponsible behaviors repeats herself; "I said watch out for the kids." The boy driving answered her back, "I don't see any kids." As soon as he said that the passengers points at the two children. "Hey man, there they go."

The children oblivious to the danger they were in rides on eventually clearing the car totally. Then the driver peaks his head out the window and started yelling at the kids, "Didn't your mama tell ya'll about riding behind cars when they backing up." Shayla then angrily answer back for the children, "Didn't your mama teach you not to drink and drive." Shayla turned around and gathered her composer before she knocked on the door. All the while Nandi, after hearing the commotion outside, watched everything that happened from the kitchen window. Shayla knocked on the door; Nandi answered it, and asked Shayla, "Is everything all right?"

"Hi, Mrs. Johnson. Yes, everything is fine; it was just those two idiots across the street almost ran over two kids because they were too drunk to pay attention to what they were doing."

"Thank god that you were on your way here, and saw them in time. So what brings you by today, you and Jurist plan on going somewhere?"

"No Ma'am, I came by to tell you all some fantastic news. Mr. Sharrieff just told me that he got both Jurist and I scholarships to The State of Florida University."

"Is that the college you all planned to attend?"

"Not really, I wanted to go to a historical black college, but to get a four year scholarship to any school is a blessing."

"Yes, it is. I'm sure Jurist is going to be very happy to hear the news. He's in his room reading. You can go on back there to tell him just knock on the door first. "Shayla, congratulations I'm proud of you." Nandi told Shayla as she gave her a rewarding hug. Shayla then walked back to Jurist's room and knocked on the door. "Come in!" Jurist shouted. When he saw Shayla open the door, a big smile stretches across his face. "What's up baby? Come here."

Shayla feeling totally opposite to the emotions she had whole on the porch is engulfed with joy as she walked over to sit besides Jurist on the bed. Shayla is very anxious, as she got ready to tell Jurist the news. "Guess what?"

"What?"

"I just left Mr. Sharrieff's house, and he told me that he was able to get us both, four-year scholarships to the State of Florida University."

"For real! How?"

"I don't know, I didn't ask. But he wants us to have dinner at his place tonight to celebrate." Although Jurist isn't looking sad, Shayla isn't getting the vibe she expected from Jurist. "What's wrong baby, you don't seem as thrilled as I thought you would be. Talk to me what's the matter?"

"I, I'm just shocked. I mean I can understand him managing to get you a scholarship but how was he able to get me one too. I only scored 21 on the ACT, and my GPA is a 2.9."

"Baby, you improved a lot your last two years, colleges look at those sorts of things. Not to mention that you won the Brain Bowl your senior year, and became senior class president. Baby, you're a born leader, and maybe that's what Mr. Sharrieff told them."

"I guess you're right."

"Aren't I always? Well, I'll meet you at Mr. Sharrieff's house later. I have to go to the store, and tell my mom."

"You want me to go with you?"

"No, you stay here and talk to your mom about it. I'll see you later." Shayla leaned over kisses Jurist then got up off the bed, and walked out of the room. As she walked towards the door, she waves at Nandi who is sitting at the kitchen table, listening to the radio, and cutting coupons, "By Mrs. Johnson."

"By Shayla, tell your mother I said hi."

"I will."

As Shayla closed the door, Nandi stopped what she's doing, and walked to Jurist room.

"Shayla told you the news?"

"Yeah, she told me. So what you think ma?"

"Baby, I just want you to do what makes you happy."

"I wish I could tell Ermine."

"You haven't heard anything new yet from his mother or anybody?"

"Nope, she said she just hope he turned himself in before a policeman try to make a name for himself, and kill Ermine in the process."

"I'll continue to pray for him, and that's the best thing any of us can do."

Chapter 14
Irony

NIGHTFALL HAS COME, and Jurist is on his way to Mr. Sharrieff's house where Shayla is awaiting him. As he walked through the darkness, Jurist only has the company of lights from illuminating stars, a crescent moon, and a few street lamps that brightens his path. Thoughts of Ermine running, and dodging police like a Wild West outlaw feverishly attack his mind. Although for him, the prospect of school, and the possibility for a better life are virtually right behind the next door. This image does little to solace the psychological pain he suffers while enduring the lost of his closest friend. Jurist struggled to find an appeasing face, and joyous attitude, to showcase before he knocked on the door and enter Mr. Sharrieff's home.

Mr. Sharrieff answered the door with a large smile, and guarded enthusiasm. "Jurist, good to see you. How have you been?"
"I've been ok. Thanks for the invitation."

"Shayla's in the kitchen preparing dinner. Come, follow me to the living room." Mr. Sharrieff leads Jurist to his contemporary, bachelorized living room. "Have a seat." He told Jurist as he sat down in his garnet leather reclining chair. "Jurist, I'm going to get right to the point. Have you made up your mind about the State of Florida University?"

Candidly Jurist replied, "To be honest, I'm still in shock actually. It's just that I'm trying to figure out how you managed to get me a four-year scholarship."

"Jurist, I didn't get you anything, you earned it. Jurist you have to understand that there are people in this world who are very successful, that probably wouldn't be as successful if they had to endure half of what you have had to endure. I simply explained your situation to the scholarship committee, and provided them with examples of your potential."

"Thanks Mr. Sharrieff, if it weren't for you, and Shayla I don't know where I would be right now, and I mean that."

"Jurist, I was only doing my job. You choose to walk the path. You put in the extra study time, not me. You deserve this opportunity because you, through all the obstacles in your life, you persevered, and continue to strive. That type of fortitude is what makes a man a man."

"Thank you Mr. Sharrieff, I appreciate your kind words."

"This is the only way it should be, brothers helping one another. One day you'll be a bridge builder for the next generation of young brothers, and sisters. If given the chance wouldn't you do the same?"

"Of course I would."

"We are a part of a long lineage of individuals that were willing to lay down their lives to help others. Men like Toussaint L'Ouveture," Mr. Sharrieff stood up from his seat, and walked over to his wall that's covered with numerous Black leaders, "Marcus Garvey, Malcolm X, and countless others who put the lives of others before their own. All because they saw the truth, the saw the light, they saw the systems that oppressed them for what they were, but they didn't stop there because they felt it necessary to expose the systems for others to see. But most importantly their combined knowledge left a blueprint for all of us to follow. Your father lived by the science, and pretence of those very same values."

Gently Jurist utter, "But look at the good that did him."

"Jurist I never told you this before because I didn't think it was appropriate, but I was there the day your father was assassinated, and although I was young I knew he believed in his plight, and he sought out to open the eyes of others including yours. That day he in both his life, and death opened the eyes of this entire community. But my question to you is, if given the opportunity would you choose to walk that path like your father, and the men before him?"

"With all due respect Mr. Sharrieff no, no I wouldn't. If my memory serves me correctly, all those men you keep referring to were either betrayed, killed or both, leaving their families, and many others to grieve their deaths. So, I think I'm going to have to create a new blueprint, one that teaches us how to expand our ideas, methods, and schemes which at least helps us avoid being killed."

Mr. Sharrieff began to start laughing, and Shayla galloped from the kitchen

"Mr. Sharrieff, turn on the T.V. The police have arrested Ermine."

The reporter from the television reports, "Orange County sheriffs arrested Ermine Brown today for allegedly murdering his stepfather John Putman four weeks ago. He will be held in the Orange County Jail until he's transferred back to Palm Beach County."

"Jurist, are you ok?" Shayla asked in a motherly voice.

Mr. Sharrieff wanting to talk to Jurist alone asked Shayla to give him, and Jurist a second.

Shayla hugs Jurist, and kisses him on his check before leaving the room, "Baby, I'm going to go upstairs, and get ready for dinner. I'll be right back."

"Jurist you've made great progress in your life, I would hate for you to regress because of Ermines misfortune. Sometimes you just have to learn how to let go."

"Let go, let go. What happened to all that talk about brothers being brothers, and helping one another? Ermine's misfortune is the same as mine. But you don't have to worry. Enough people have told me, the only way I can help him is to continue to progress yourself."
"Do you think he should go to jail for what he did?"

Anger overcame Jurist's composer, and he exploded, "Hell nall, his step-dad deserved exactly what he got. But I don't think Ermine should have had to do what he allegedly did. He shouldn't have had to grow up in that mess of a family. If that had been my mother, and my step-dad, I would have tried to put a stop to that years ago."

"What, you think it's ok to kill another man because you have a disagreement with him?"

"Ermines life remained day in and day out in immediate danger. Some crimes are just as wrong as murder; therefore the penalty should be the same."

Calmly, Mr. Sharrieff reiterate his position with a short anecdote, "There was once a group of beings called Gods who shared the very same ideology as you, but they were removed from their primordial positions. However, Professor Conan is trying to reunite these beings, and return them to their original grace."

"Who is Professor Conan? What he got to do with me and Ermine."

"He is one of the contributors of the scholarships Shayla, and you will be receiving. He is a good brother, and a well-educated man. I have two plane tickets for you, and Shayla to fly to Tallahassee to meet with him, and others who want to see who they will be investing their funds and time into."

Jurist regains his composure, "I'll have to ask my mother if I can go but I don't think she'll say no."

"Of course, of course as a matter of fact, I would like to schedule a meeting with her sometime soon. When do you think she'll be available?"

"I don't know but when I get home I'll have her give you a call."

Shayla, finishing changing, came down stairs. "Are you guys ready to eat yet?"

Mr. Sharrieff answered, "Yes, I'm starved and the food smells delicious Li sis." Mr. Sharrieff then put his arms around Jurist,

"Come on little brother, let's go say a prayer and eat."

Chapter 15
Parental Consent

MAKING THE USUAL CLASH, AND RATTLING SOUND, WHEN IT IS OPENED, Nandi hears the screen door as it crashes against the house. She preemptively got up from her reading position, and walked towards the front door. She heard no knock at the door, assuming that it was Jurist; she slowly contemplated what to say to him because she too had heard the news of Ermines arrest. As soon as Jurist entered the door she greets him. "So how was dinner, baby?"

"It was good. Shayla cooked some wings and broccoli. Did you see the news?"

"Yes, I saw it ma."

"I figured that you had already seen it. Baby, I'm so sorry, but at least we know that he's safe now."

"Safe, I wouldn't exactly call being locked up safe. He would have been safer if they had left him alone. But I'm okay, Mr. Sharrieff and I talked about it. By the way, Mr. Sharrieff wants you to call him."

"What for?"

"He wants Shayla and I to fly to Tallahassee to meet with a couple professors. So he told me to ask you to give him a call."
"I'll go call him now."

Nandi walked to her room to call Mr. Sharrieff, as she tried to decide for herself if she feels this trip is a good idea. For some reason she is still reluctant to trust Mr. Sharrieff.

"Hello, may I speak to Mr. Sharrieff?"

"Speaking."

"Hi, this is Mrs. Johnson."

"How are you doing tonight Mrs. Johnson? I'm glad you call."

"I'm doing, thanks for asking. I called because Jurist told me that you want him to fly to Tallahassee to meet with some professors."

"Yes, Professor Conan, and some of the other professors, and contributors are throwing a banquet in recognition of this year scholarship recipients. This is simply an opportunity for recipients, and the contributors to get together to get to know one another."
"What about supervision? Are they going to have a chaperone?" Nandi asked.

"They'll have an escort that will make sure they get from the airport, and to anywhere else they need to go but no they will not be under constant supervision."

"Well, who's going to watch over him when he's not at a scheduled event?"

"Mrs. Johnson, please take no offense to what I'm about to say. Jurist is a young man now. He's going to have to learn to fend for himself soon. You did an excellent job rearing him and I think he's responsible enough to make sure he gets to bed, and get up on time. However, he will have numbers to call if he needs anything."

"Mr. Sharrieff, I'm sorry if I sound over protective but Jurist is my all, and I don't want anything to happen to him."

"Believe me Mrs. Johnson. Jurist will be treated like he's all we have as well. You have my word on that."

"How long will he be gone?"

"Only for the weekend."

"What did Shayla's mother say about this trip?"

"She has already signed her permission slip. While we're on the subject of Shayla, I don't know if Jurist told you or not but I am Shayla's brother. We have the same father but different mothers. We decided not to tell anyone because Shayla has taken two of my class. I am telling you this because I want you to know that you can trust me, and that I truly want to see Jurist do well in life. Especially since it seems as though, my little sister is head over heels in love with him."

"Mr. Sharrieff, I know I may come off as if I'm unappreciative of your efforts to help Jurist but I am..." Mr. Sharrieff cuts Mrs. Johnson off before she could finish verbalizing her thought.

"Don't worry about it Mrs. Johnson it's your job to be a little apprehensive you are his mother. I'll send a permission slip to you by Jurist."

"All right, you have a good night Mr. Sharrieff."

"You have a good night as well Mrs. Johnson."

Chapter 16
The Flight

AFTER FLYING AMONGST THE HEAVENS, Shayla, and Jurist land in the capital city of Florida. Flowing with its canopy landscape and multicultural educational attainment facilities, Tallahassee is a member of Leon County: A county that less than a hundred, and fifty years ago lead the region in White to Slave ratio, with 351 slaves to every 100 white persons. Now known as a breeding ground for philosophers, scholars, and politicians; small town people like Jurist and Shayla are sure to benefit from the historic edification and neo-culture of this small city. When Shayla and Jurist arrive at the airport Shayla reminds Jurist to look for their guide Amos, who is suppose to be waiting for them. "Jurist, make sure you don't overlook the sign."

"There he is there." Jurist points to the 6-foot naturally built, clean shaved brother with the State of Florida University shirt on. Amos is an intellectual conversationalist with the vocabulary of a poet. He's very well organized, and has impeccable taste, he always wears his shirt tucked in, and he often carries a notepad. They walked over to meet the greeter who's come to guide them through this city of knowledge.

"Shayla and Jurist I presume."

"How are you doing?" Shayla said as she smiled and greets him. "So, I guess you're Amos." Jurist speaks in a voice a little fervent voice.

"That is I, and I am him. Here's a copy of the itinerary. If you have any questions just ask."

Shayla eager to meet the man responsible for their escape from the routine of small town living, she asked. "When are we going to meet Professor Conan?"

"We're going to meet with Professor Conan, and the others, at *Jasper's* for lunch."

"Amos, where you from?" Jurist asked in his southern slang. "I'm from D.C. I'm a graduate student, and I also work as Professor Conan's program assistant." After they get to know one another they all head to the car expeditiously.

Soon they arrive at the restaurant. Upon their entrance they immediately spot the professors' table. It was easy to tell which table belonged to the professors because they were the only people sitting at a table arraigned to seat three additional people. At the head of the table, Professor Conan talked to a male and female colleague about state school policies.

"Yes, we need to put a committee together to watch the progress of the program."

Amos approaches the table with Shayla and Jurist behind him. "Excuse me ladies, and gentlemen; I'll like to introduce you all to Shayla Courtland and Jurist Johnson."

Jurist speaks first, "Hello everyone." Ensued by a response by Shayla.

"Nice to meet all of you."

"It's my pleasure to meet both of you. Professor Conan said cordially before he introduces the others esteemed individuals seated at the table. "I am Professor Omar Conan, and this is my wife Ebony. Next to her is Dr. Quentin Woodrow. Mr. Woodrow is Dean of undergraduate studies."

Mr. Woodrow greets Jurist and Shayla, and then he extends an invitation to them both, "If you all need help with anything make sure to contact me." Professor Conan then reached over, and passes them both a menu. "Feel free to order whatever you like."

"Thank you, that's very generous Professor." Soon after Jurist thanks Professor Conan he quickly explores the menu.

Professor Conan being the cunning yet straight forward guy he is soon switches the subject to a more academic conversation. "Have you all decided what field of study you're planning to major in?"

Shayla already secure in her answer replies, "I would like to double major in English, and African-American history."

Jurist a little more reserved, and indecisive followed Shayla remarks with a more board answer, "I was thinking about being a lawyer."

One could tell by the expression on Professor Conan's face that Jurist answer was a little too broad, and grammatically incorrect. So he asked him more specifically? "What type of lawyer would you like to become?" Jurist had never given any thought to becoming one specific type of lawyer, and since his linguistics was one that some people have linked to ebonics. He thought like most kids his age; that a lawyer is a lawyer, and he saw nothing wrong with saying being instead of becoming. So he simply responds, "I ain't decided yet." Dean Quentin Woodrow quickly recognized that Jurist wasn't prepared for this type of discussion, and smoothly interjects with a comforting commentary. "Well, don't worry we'll help you decide."

Then Mr. Conan sat straight up in his seat and said, "Yes, if either of you have any problems or questions don't be afraid to speak up, and ask questions. Remember we are here to help you."

Shayla answered back with the smile of a slave, "We will remember that Mrs. Conan. Thank you for the offer." Jurist follows up with a routine reactive thank you.

When Jurist and Shayla finally make it to the hotel, Shayla walked over to the air conditioner, and turned the knob to high cool. "Ah that feels good." She stretches, and yawns, "I didn't think it would be so hot up here." Amos realizing that Jurist and Shayla had a tiresome day, he looked at Jurist and said, "I hope you all had fun today."

Jurist picks up the remote, and turned on the television, "We did, and we appreciate the entire tour of the campus. We know you had other things you could have been doing with your time."

"Believe me it was no problem man."

Shayla walked to the sink in the back, "Hey Amos, you sure we don't have anything else on the itinerary."

"Not until tomorrow night's scholarship banquet."

"That's great because I don't want to walk another foot. My feet are killing me, and my hair is a mess."

"Who you telling, my feet are killing me too." Jurist sighed, and lay back on the bed.

Amos walking back towards the door, "Well, I'm going to let you all be, I have to go, and finish typing this report, but I'll be by to pick you all up for breakfast at eight a.m. sharp tomorrow morning."

Shayla peaks her head up from the sink, and grabbed a towel. "Thanks for your help today Amos, we really enjoyed ourselves."

"If ya'll need anything my home, and pager number is on the card I put on the table by the phone."

Jurist got up from the bed, and walked over to Amos, "Hey Amos, let me talk to you for a minute before you leave." They both walked outside of the hotel room. "Amos, I want you to be honest with me. At lunch today, what did I do wrong?"

Jurist you did nothing wrong, that's just how Professor Conan is. The students around campus call him Professor X because of his militant style of teaching, and hard grading curve. Trust me when I tell you, it's not you it's him. He always expects perfection. Now don't get me wrong, he's a good man, and great professor. It's just that he's tuff; especially on the people he expects to have the most potential. But with all that being said, he's still a fair man. My advice to you is, be yourself. You're a smart brother. But it's not Professor Conan that you have to prove it to. You have to prove that to yourself. It's just that proving it to Professor Conan helps you prove it to yourself."

"Thanks Amos, I appreciate the advice."

"No problem brother, that's what I'm here for."

Jurist walked back into the room, and Shayla rushed right into his arms, "I had so much fun today. I can't wait until we graduate."

"Yeah, I did have fun."

"So what were you and Amos talking about?"

"Just some guy stuff."

Shayla backed up, and pulled Jurist back to the area where the beds are, "It must have been some serious guy stuff if you had to walk outside to talk about it."

Jurist pushed Shayla on the bed, and changed the subject. "How long am I going to be able to stay in your room tonight?"

"Well, that depends on how well you behave yourself."

"Suppose I told you that the bathtub is a Jacuzzi, and that downstairs they sell candles, and bubble bath."

"Then I would ask you why was that stuff downstairs, and not upstairs with us."

Jurist and Shayla start kissing, and rolling all over the bed. Then Shayla stopped him abruptly. "Hold up lover boy. What about the bubble bath and candles?"

Jurist jumped up from the bed, "I'll be back in two minutes."

"You better make it one minute, I might change my mind in two." Jurist rushed out the door as Shayla giggled and smiled.

Meanwhile, Professor Conan is on the phone with Mr. Sharrieff. Mr. Sharrieff is sitting at his desk inside his study. "Where are they now?" He asked Professor Conan.

"Amos recently called, and informed me that he had dropped them off at the hotel."

"So tell me, what type of impression did he leave upon you?"

"He seems a little timid, and indecisive."

"Trust me Omar, he's not timid at all, he was probably just a little nervous. This was his first trip away from home without his mom."

"Abdul, I only think it's fair to tell you that the council has been looking at another candidate in Arkansas."

"I'm not worried, they can look all they want but mark my words.

Jurist is the one."

"For all of our sakes I hope he is because our time is running short."

"Omar just talk to him you'll see his potential, and I'm not talking all your psycho mumbo jumbo bull. Just be real with him."

"Progress through Knowledge"

"Prosperity through Freedom"

Shayla and Jurist still wet from the Jacuzzi are curled besides one another on the bed. Neither of them is talking to one another but both of them are deep in concentration.

Then after a while Jurist came out of nowhere and said, "I'm going to ask him tomorrow."

Shayla confused by Jurist statement, "Ask who, what?"

"Professor. Conan," he exclaims, "I'm going to ask him why they chose me."

"Jurist, baby you trippin for real now. Who cares why they picked you?"

"I do, I have a strange feeling that something's not right. It's something somebody isn't telling me. I can feel it."

"I'm sorry baby, but I thought you would have been thinking about feeling something other than why some people chose you to get a scholarship." Shayla got out of the bed, and put on her shoes.

"Jurist, we away from our folks, and in the city that we are about to attend college. Don't spoil this weekend by asking everyone a bunch of stupid questions, and ruin a great evening. I'm going to the snack room, and when I return either be really romantic or don't be here at all."

Chapter 17
The Banquet

IT'S A BEAUTIFUL NIGHT IN TALLAHASSEE. The stars fill the sky as they play hide, and seek with the moon. The wind gently kisses the leaves of unsuspecting pine trees. All around the air smells like a fruity perfume, especially at the round hotel where the New Futures Association Annual Scholarship banquet is being held. Some of the most prominent, and affluent people in the nation are in attendance. Islands of achievement fill the elaborate golden room were some of the states brightest achievers are accepting scholarships to some of the top ranked schools of higher education within the Atlantic Region of the nation.

The host speaker Mrs. Jane Donell, president of a local bank is just about to give Shayla her scholarship certificate. "This year we have two NFA recipients from Belle Glade. Our first recipient is Shayla Courtland." The crowd remains seated while they applaud Shayla, as she made her way toward the podium. "Shayla on behalf of the New Future Association I am proud to award you this scholarship certificate for your excellence in academic achievement, and a plaque to commemorate your four year scholarship to the State of Florida University." Everyone started to applaud, then Shayla took the mic, "I just want to say thank you, thank you all, and God bless." Shayla walked away as gracefully as she had walked up to the podium with the sound of fading applauds at her back. With triumphant strides, she returned to her seat. Mrs. Donell took her place back at the helm. "Our final scholarship recipient tonight is Mr. Jurist Johnson." As Jurist started making his way towards the podium like clockwork, everyone began applauding.

When Jurist arrived at the podium applauds subside, and Mrs. Donell said, "Congratulations Jurist, would you like to share any words with us?"

Jurist stood behind the podium, and glanced over the sea of beings that he believe to be his people and said, "As I look out into the crowd, I must say this is one of the most beautiful sights I have ever had the privilege to bear witness to. It's so great to see a group of individuals much like me, in appearance, and stature who are willing, and able to extend a hand out to help a fellow brother and sister.

After all, this is what it's all about isn't it. Since the day I was told I was receiving a NFA scholarship, I've wondered why me. But now that I'm here I not only see why, I feel why. Your spirits radiate a belief in the progression of the black community. So, I gladly accept your scholarship, and give you my word that I will not let you down. Thank you."

Jurist raised his plaque above his head, stood there for a couple of seconds shining in the midst of a standing ovation before returning to his seat. When he reached his seat, the applauding faded, and Shayla whispered into his ear, "You always got to show out ha?"

Moments before everyone stopped clapping, Mrs. Donell asked the attendees for another round of applause for this year's scholarship recipients. After the applause, everyone embark to mingle amongst each other. In the meantime, Professor Conan walked through a crowd of congratulations to reach Jurist's table. When he finally manages to reach Jurist, he asked Jurist to follow him. Outside under the light of the gray sun, Professor Conan put his hand on Jurist shoulder as a father would do a son, and told him how great his acceptance speech was. Jurist modestly turned down Professor Conan's praises for the speech because he felt he was only saying what he felt. He saw it only as an opportunity to say what he felt at that point in time.

Professor Conan still astounded by the words that moved the entire association wondered where Jurist learned to speak with such passion and conviction. So he asked, and Jurist's response to him was that he probably got it from his father, as if it was a hereditary gene.

Professor Conan uttered, "The rare talent for public speaking is a real gift, and many prominent men have gained such status because of a gift such as yours." Although Professor Conan knew that the ability to inspire could be a very powerful tool, he felt Jurist lacked the confidence in his inspirational ability. Jurist you have the gift of inspiration.

"Who can I inspire?" Jurist asked. "People like you are the ones that give me inspiration." For a moment they both stood dormant in thought as if time had slowed down just for them. Professor Conan then explains to Jurist why both his presence, and words, moved him and others. He wanted Jurist to understand the significance of a person that has the ability to both shock and awe groups of listeners. "The power to look at the crowd, and speak to all as if you're talking to each person individually is the power of an ordained being, that's the power you possess. The ability to pierce a man or a woman's heart, mind and soul with just words can be more powerful than any gun. You are a special young man Jurist, and soon you will realize how special."

Inside of the banquet room, Shayla walked over to say 'hi' to Mrs. Conan who is sitting alone sipping on a glass of white wine admiring the elegance of the night. It doesn't take long for her to invite Shayla to have a seat, and partake in a friendly conversation. After a little small talk about the awards, and future plans in college, they soon begin to talk about the relationship Shayla shares with Jurist. "You and Jurist seem very close, much closer than just regular schoolmates."

"What gave you that impression?" Shayla responds with a staggered look on her face.

"I was your age once. I can tell by the way you look at him."

Shayla began to blush because she knew what Mrs. Conan was saying was true. She just didn't think that her feelings for Jurist could be so obvious to a total stranger.

"I'm not getting to personal am I? Maybe you would prefer me to be like most of the others around here, and talk about meaningless ideas filled with impersonal statements that divulge nothing about whom we are. If you are one of the ones in a mad race to speak empty rhetoric to everyone in the room before you leave, don't let me stop you. I just thought that I saw something different in you."

Stunned by the straight forwardness of Mrs. Conan, Shayla tried to decide her next course of action. Mrs. Conan helps her out, "So, tell me about you and Jurist. I just love, love stories."

Shayla then relaxes, and began talking, "I don't tell him but when I'm around him I feel both safe and nervous all at the same time."

Mrs. Conan gently places her hand on the top of Shayla's hand.

"Some people say that's one of the initial symptoms of love."

"But we're not old enough to be in love are we?"

Mrs. Conan then crosses her legs, and turned her body directly towards Shayla. "Girl, love knows no age. It's the commitment to one another that takes growth, and maturity. As long as you respect yourself, he will respect you. It seems to me that he's a respectable young man with goals, and drive, and I'm willing to bet that he's already head over heels in love with you. Boys and men just need a strong woman to help them stay on the golden path. You have to remember Shayla, women are, and will always be the grand treasure of man; a gift from God put here to guide men to righteousness."

"He better stay on my path or I might have to kill him."
They both start to giggle and smile.

"Girl, I heard that!"

"How old were you and Professor Conan when you knew you all were in love, and wanted to get married."

"I was nineteen, and he was twenty-one, but times were different then. We were a closer group of people then, with a clear mission, and sense of duty. Your generation is growing up in a totally different world then the one we grew up in."

"That's true, Shayla responds. "I think we have to deal with more perceptional deceptions and separateness."

"Shayla, I was thinking that since tonight's your last night here, how about you and Jurist come stay with us. We can get up in morning, and I can show you some pictures of Professor Conan and I when we were younger, and if you don't mind you can help me prepare breakfast."

"That's very nice of you Mrs. Conan, Jurist and I would be honored to stay with you and Professor Conan. As a matter of fact, I'll go tell Jurist now. Excuse me."

Shayla got up from the table, and walked through the crowded banquet room searching for Jurist. Then she spots him talking to another one of the recipients. "Jurist, Jurist, excuse me." She said to the recipient who just happens to be a stunning young lady with hazel eyes, and caramel-brown skin draped in an eye catching silk even gown, which in Shayla's opinion, is too close up on Jurist. "Jurist, Mrs. Conan invited us to stay with them tonight."

Jurist being careful to make sure that he doesn't provoke any hostility or misunderstanding from Shayla introduces the Chicago native to Shayla.

"I'm sorry Isis, this is Shayla. Shayla this is Isis Nahash."

Isis took a quick glance at Shayla and said, "Nice to meet you."

"Yeah, nice to meet you as well." Shayla replies in an disdainful voice, "Jurist we need to find Amos so we can go to the hotel and check out."

Jurist completely unaware of the plans that Shayla has made for him and her, he excuses himself from Isis presence, and walked a couple feet back to talk to Shayla.

"Why are you acting so rude, and what's going on."

"Well excuse me, but we need to find Amos."

"What do we need to go to their house for? I like staying at the hotel. I thought you liked staying there too." Jurist walked closer to Shayla in a more seductive manner.

"If you want to you can stay at the hotel. Maybe you can talk Isis into staying there with you. But I'm going to stay at Mr. and Mrs. Conan's house tonight."

Jurist totally unprepared, and defenseless against Shayla's verbal onslaught, he took a big sigh and said, "Shayla you have got to be kidding me."

"Jurist." Shayla now employs a much softer tone. "Come on, let's go find Amos. I really want to stay at the Conan's house to night. Please."

Jurist walked over to Isis, "It was very nice meeting you, I'm sorry we can't continue our conversation but something urgent has come up."

"No problem, Isis smiled at Jurist, I'll see you later."

As soon as Shayla and Jurist find Amos, they instruct him of their need to get to the hotel to pack so they can go spend the night at the Conan's house. On the way to the house Amos briefs them on the little history that he knows of Omar and Ebony Conan. "You all must have made a good impression. They never invite people to stay at their home. I myself have never been invited to stay although I have visited on numerous occasions."

"Do they have any children of their own?" Shayla inquires.

"They have a son but he's locked up. He got caught riding down to Miami with some friends of his. One of the guys had half a kilo of cocaine in his bag."

That's when Jurist interest arose, "Was it his?" Until then he rode in the car silent, and exclusive in his thoughts about tonight.

"He said it wasn't but the State gave him seven years anyway. That was big news up here. They even tried to say that Professor Conan was involved because the hotel, and the rental car were reserved in his name."

"Damn that's messed up," is all Jurist thought about as he contemplated the ordeal.

When they arrived at the Conan's house, Amos got out and rang the doorbell three times before Mrs. Conan came to answer it. "I'm glad you all came. Thank you for bringing them Amos."

"No problem Mrs. Conan. I'll see you all tomorrow, Goodnight."

"Thanks again, Amos. Jurist and I really do appreciate your endless hospitality."

"No problem. Goodnight all." He then turned from the door, and walked to his car to leave while Jurist and Shayla followed Mrs. Conan into the house.

"You and your husband have a beautiful home Mrs. Conan. Did you decorate it yourself?"

"Thank you, Shayla. Yes I did, all except for Omar's study. As a matter of fact Jurist, Omar is in there now; it's down the hall to your right. You'll hear the music playing. Leave your bags here I'll take them to your room. Come with me Shayla I'll show you the rest of the house."

Jurist walked down the hall but as he is walking he notice portraits of African kingdoms and monuments. When he entered the room Professor Conan is sitting in a leather reclining chair with his back to the door. Jurist then observes a small collection of slave pictures, and framed newspaper clippings of blacks being lynched, and civil rights activist.

Then a voice came from the chair. "Do you like my study?"

"I must say it's very interesting."

"What do you mean by interesting?"

"It's nothing really. I just noticed that when I was walking down the hall there were pictures of kings, and monuments but in here there aren't any. There are only pictures of slaves, and lynching, and people being beat as they marched."

"Do you think I arranged them in that manner deliberately?"

"Almost everything is done deliberately." Jurist looked directly into Professor Conan's face as he spoke. "It looked to me like it's some sort of timeline."

"Very good, Mr. Johnson!" Professor Conan rises up out of his seat.

"Come with me; let's take a trip through time."

They walked out the door, and back to the beginning of the hallway, and Professor Conan started explaining each individual portrait. "First we have here a picture of Ethiopia, and monuments in Harar. Second, we have the founder of the Dynastic Kemet. Before Professor Conan could finish revealing the name of the individual to whom he was referring to Jurist interjects. "King Narmer."

"Yes it is. I see you have a little historical knowledge." Professor Conan then points to the third portrait, "This is the world first so-called genius Imhotep. Imhotep was an architect, astronomer, philosopher, poet, and physician all of which are professions you should aspire to comprehend." Professor Conan and Jurist walked to the next picture. "This is one of the, if not the greatest general, and military strategist who ever lived, "The Ruler of Carthage."

Jurist interjects again, "I agree with him being a great general but military strategist he was not. If he had been a better strategist he wouldn't have been defeated by the Romans."

It brought Professor Conan great pleasure to know that Jurist was as big a fan of history as he is. "I know you know who this king is."

Jurist replies, "Shaka Zulu, King of the Zulus. A great king that could not escape the misconceived prophesies of his birth; which in-turn brought fourth his early demise. In the thickest mist of the plot to crucify him he said what I think were the truest, and most profound words, that anybody ever spoke, when you kill me the white man will come, and make slaves of all of you. But my question to you Professor Conan is out of all the millions of pictures you could have chose; why did you pick these portraits over the countless of others?"

"That's a very good question Jurist. These men, and kingdoms, represent the true nature of courage, intelligence, unity, ingenuity, and leadership. Not to mention that they used their power to

105

protect their people through cultural protection. Come on; let's go back to the study."

Perplexed, he asked Professor Conan, "Why do you intentionally surround yourself with all this negativity and violence?

"I don't try to surround myself with negativity. I merely surround myself with the truth. This is our not so distant past." Professor Conan walked over, and points to an illustration of a slave auction. "This is our present." He points at a picture of a civil rights march. "And this is where I try to help create a more positive future for our people." Professor Conan walked over to his desk, and sat in his comfortable chair, as would a king on his throne. It would have to be comfortable because no man could tolerate spending so much time in such a mentally laborious room without at least the pleasure of a cozy, secure throne to sit upon.

"You say that you sit here in this room, and think of ways for our people to have better lives. How do you plan to do that if you surround yourself in so much degradation and strife?"

"Because it's what drives me to never quit making sure brothers and sisters, like you and Shayla, have as many opportunities as others within this nation to succeed."

"What type of opportunities do you feel are necessary for us to have?"

"True freedom, which includes economic and political empowerment, of course." Professor Conan looked at his grandfather clock as it struck 2:00 AM. "Man it's late. Let me walk you to your room so you can get some sleep."

Jurist fascinated by the fact that he actually believed that Professor Conan was willfully trying to better the people, and not just himself. He pondered for a second then he asked Professor Conan if it was okay if he stayed, and talked with him for a little while longer. Professor Conan himself was touched by Jurist willingness to stay up, and talk about the problems of the world.   But not only did Jurist want to talk about the problems, he gave critical and astute insight into ways to improve cultural pitfalls. So the two stayed up half the night talking about things that have affected the entire globe from the beginning of time.

When morning came Shayla knocked on the door of Jurist's room but he did not answer her. So she opened the door, and slowly peeked through the crack. When she noticed that Jurist was still in the bed lying down. She swiftly walked over to him.

"Jurist, Jurist, wake up. Get your stuff ready Amos is here."

Completely shocked by Shayla's interference of the little sleep that he was trying to get, Jurist sat up almost franticly, "What, what happen?" He said as his heartbeat doubled. Shayla sitting by his side answered, "Nothing silly, you and Professor Conan must have stayed up all last night."

Jurist got up and walked to the restroom to wash his face. "Why didn't you knock? You're not supposed to sneak up on people in their sleep like that. You can give a person a heart attack."

"I did knock but you didn't want to get up mister sleepy head."

Jurist opened his mouth wide, took a big yawn, and stared at himself in the mirror. "What you waking me up this early for anyway."

"Boy it's not early; it's almost 10:30 a.m. We were about to begin eating breakfast. Professor Conan said that you probably wanted to sleep through but I decided to come get you up anyway."

"Well, I'll be there after I finish brushing my teeth, and packing my things away."

"All right, I'm going to go back out to the kitchen, and let everyone know we can begin without Prince Jurist."

When Jurist finally made it to the kitchen, he came in with his bag in his hand. Mrs. Conan instructs him to put his bags in the car, and come back to the kitchen to eat. "I'll have your plate ready by time you get back."

Jurist walked to the car, and put his things in the trunk, and walked back to the kitchen. And like she said she had his plate ready.

Jurist sat at the table, "Good morning everybody."

They almost simultaneously replied, "Good morning."
Mrs. Conan asked him, "Did you have a nice sleep Jurist?"

Jokingly Shayla butt in, "I hope so I heard him snoring all the way in my room."

Jurist looked over to Shayla as if to say shut up. "Yes I did Mrs. Conan."

Professor Conan who is reading the morning paper at the table folds it down and said, "I hope you all enjoyed your visit?"
Shayla responds as she began to pick up a glass of orange juice, "This was one of the best trips I've ever been on." Then she took a sip.

Jurist looked around the table and said, "Yeah, we can't thank you all enough for your hospitality. By the way, we need the address to the New Futures Association that way we can send them a thank you letter."

Professor Conan reached into his shirt pocket, and pulled out one of his personal business cards, "Here, take my card, and send it to the address below."

Jurist grabbed the card, and places it in his rear right pants pocket. Then he regains his focus on the food in front of him, but before Jurist demolish the well-prepared breakfast, he bows his head to pray. "Lord, we would just like to thank you for the many blessings you have bestowed upon us. We would like to thank you for this nurturing food, and beautiful day. We also ask that you protect us, and our loved ones, as we travel life corridors to reach the heavens that you call home. All of these things we ask in your name. Amen."

Within minutes Jurist cleans his plate, and asked to be excused from the table to call his mother. Mrs. Conan instructs him to go use the phone in Professor Conan study.

Meanwhile, Nandi is already on the phone with Mr. Sharrieff.

"Mr. Sharrieff, I was just calling to make sure that you were going to pick Jurist, and Shayla up from the airport."

"Yes, Mrs. Johnson I was planning on leaving to pick them up at 1:30 p.m. So, how are you doing?"

"I'm okay I'm just a little anxious to see Jurist. I tried calling his room but he didn't answer. Then the people at the front desk said that he had already checked out."

Nandi's phone beeps, and interrupts Mr. Sharrieff just as he was about to speak.

Mr. Sharrieff let me call you back I have someone calling me on the other line, it maybe him calling now. Nandi, flashes to the other line. "Hello." As she had suspected it was Jurist. "Ma!"

"Boy I just got off the phone with Mr. Sharrieff. I tried calling your room why didn't you answer the phone."

"I forgot to tell the hotel people to give you the number to Professor Conan's house. We stayed with him and his wife last night. As a matter of fact, we've just finished eating breakfast. I was just calling you because I knew you had probably called the room, and started to worry like usual."

"Jurist you could have at least called me to let me know that you were going over there."

"Ma, everything happened so fast, and it was late. Not to mention that I just got up thirty minutes ago."

"Alright Jurist it's just that I got a little nervous. You know me. I was on the phone with Mr. Sharrief when you called. He said he's going to pick you and Shayla up from the airport. I'll see you when you get in. I love you."

"I love you to ma; I'll see you when I get back."

Jurist walked back to the table, and finish drinking his orange juice. Understanding the worries that mothers have for their children, Mrs. Conan asked Jurist if everything was okay with his mother.

"Yes, everything's fine Mrs. Conan thanks for asking."

Shayla walked over and collects Jurist's plate.

Full and charmed by Shayla's gracious service, Jurist thanks Mrs. Conan for the delicious food.

"Don't thank me; Shayla did most of the cooking."

Professor Conan took a quick peek from behind the newspaper to tell Shayla how excellent he thought the meal was. Soon after, the clock started to chime.

"Oh, look at the time," Mrs. Conan murmurs. "You kids need to get going. Come on, we'll walk you to the door."

Chapter 18
The Return

SHAYLA AND JURIST RETURNED TO SOUTH FLORIDA with a renewed sense of pride, and vigor that transpired in their no longer myopic eyes or vision of the world. That weekend Jurist took the great leap to start the magnificent quest to manhood, while Shayla maintained her girlish charm with the fusion of her newfound womanly mannerisms. Yet still, their transformation would go unnoticed by Mr. Sharrieff who was waiting for them at the curbside of the airport. As they made their way to baggage claim they lovingly stroked each other's hand while intermittently taking glanced around the airport. After they picked up their bags they walked outside, and were greeted by Mr. Sharrieff.

"Did you all enjoy your trip?" He asked as he grabbed the suitcase from Shayla, and placed it in the trunk of the car.

"It was a much needed get-away." Jurist answered while smiling at Shayla.

"Yeah, that had to be the best college visit a person could have." Shayla responded.

"I'm glad you all enjoyed yourselves. What was the best part of the trip?" Shayla looked to the back seat, and smiled at Jurist. Barely holding his composer he boyishly grins, "The banquet was the best part. They showed a lot of love. Man, I'll be glad when graduation day comes."

After numerous stories, and hundreds of laughs later Mr. Sharrieff reached Jurist's house.

"All right Jurist, I see you in school tomorrow."

"Yeah, I'll see you tomorrow. Shayla call me when you get home."

"All right!"

Although both Shayla and Jurist would have loved to show more affection as they parted one anotherso,s Mr. Sharrieff was present Jurist simply walked away from the car, trotted up the porch, and entered his home.

"Ma, I'm home, ma." Jurist called out.

Nandi back in her room watching television shouted, "I'm back here."

Jurist walked back to her room.

"Baby, how was your trip?"

Jurist laid in the bed beside her. "It was much better than I thought it would be. Ma, the campus was huge, computers labs where everywhere, and it has a state of the art recreational center. I really think I'm going to like it there."

"Did you have a chance to visit any of the departments for your major?"

"Ma, I did better than that. I had lunch with the Dean of

undergraduate studies, and Professor Conan is one of the top law Professors in the nation."

"Look at you Mr. Big Shot. Your father would be so proud of you."

Chapter 19
Courting Reality

A COUPLE GREAT DAYS HAVE GONE BY, Jurist and Shayla are preparing for college, and Nandi have grown much less suspicious of Mr. Sharrieff. Jurist and Mr. Sharrieff's relationship has gotten much stronger as well. Jurist has started to relish the political, and economic, discourse between him and Mr. Sharrieff. He has also taken a great liking to African-American art and African artifacts. However, this morning as nice as it was has brought bad news. While sitting at the kitchen table reading the local newspaper, Nandi noticed Ermine's name in an article. Nandi's heart jump as her anxiety builds. Unsure of how to break the news to Jurist, Nandi got out of her seat, and paced the kitchen floor as she figured out how to break the news to Jurist. With a little trepidation Nandi walked to Jurist room. Jurist laying in the bed with part of his body under the blanket, and the other half of his body completely uncovered is sound asleep as Nandi cracks open the door to his room.

"Jurist, Jurist." Nandi whispered as she peaks her head into the room. Realizing that Jurist is as slumber as a piece of wood, Nandi walked over to the bed. "Jurist, Jurist baby, wake up. I'm sorry I woke you up out of your sleep but I thought you might want to read this."

Nandi sat at the edge of the bed while Jurist sat up against his headboard to read the paper.

"What's this ma?"

"Look at the bottom left corner. There is an article about Ermine." Jurist read the paper, and learns that Ermine has been transferred to a jail in West Palm Beach, and that Ermine is scheduled for court next week. Jurist looked to his mother.

"Ma, will you take me to his trial."

"Yeah, I'll write a note to your teacher so you'll be excused."

"Thanks ma." Said Jurist as he releases a big sigh of frustration.

"Well I know you have a lot on your mind right now so I'll let you gather yourself together. When you get out of bed I'll probably be gone, but I fixed some cheese grits and eggs, and left them on the stove. You can make yourself some toast. You might want to take a shower to, it well help you feel better. I got to go check on Mrs. Clara and Ms. Janie. You know how Ms. Janie gets when she don't get her eight o'clock oatmeal."

"All right ma, I'll see you later." Nandi walked out of the room as Jurist places the newspaper on the nightstand, and pulled the cover over his entire body.

As Jurist closed his eyes, he returned back to his world of unconscious existence, and deep thought. Faintly, under the darkness of his cover, Jurist hears someone call his name. Jurist rapidly removed the cover from his head, and sat up. "Who is it?" Jurist responds to the voice.

The voice responds, "The tears you hold will fill the hole."

Jurist tried to trace where the voice is coming from, so he moves out of his bed very quietly. Jurist noticed that his window is open, and that the screen is missing. Jurist peek his head out of the window, and a white owl flies off into the deep velvet-blue sky. Jurist looked down, and saw a hole in the ground in front of his window. Jurist peers inside the hole but he saw no bottom. Beside the hole is a bucket with an envelope inside of it. Jurist climbed through his window, and grabbed the envelope from the bucket. When Jurist opened the envelope he read the letter inside. For forty days you must journey, visiting children around the world. You must first start abroad, and then make your way back home. Every day that you are gone you must collect tears from children you encounter, and pour the bucket of tears into the hole. "But how," Jurist screamed as he drops the letter back into the bucket, "How can I visit the children of the world in only forty days?" A gust of wind then blows the letter out of the bucket, and back into Jurist's hand. The letter had four words written on it, "Follow the white owl." Suddenly, the white owl that had flown away earlier reappeared on top of an adjacent home. When the white owl flew away Jurist followed it.

For the first five days, Jurist visited every child born in England who cried because they felt poor and mentally distressed. Jurist then gave the bucket to the White owl and the White owl flew the bucket to the hole. For the next five days, Jurist visited the children of Israel, who had recently lost their loved ones, and he gathered all of their tears in the bucket, and gave it to the White owl. The next ten days came upon Jurist as he traveled deep into South America. It took twenty days for Jurist to reach, and gathered the tears of the children of Africa. Finally, the last day came before Jurist, and Jurist gazed at the loads of buckets filled with tears of helpless children that he and the White owl had collected on their escapade.

Jurist began to pour the tears of the children of England into the hole. The hole hastily grew to a large puddle of greed and poverty. Jurist then commenced pouring the tears of the children of Israel and the puddle that started out as a simple hole, became a large pond of grief and insecurity. Numerous buckets of tears later,

Jurist commenced to pouring in the tears of the children of South America. Jurist quickly noticed that the pond that once was a simple puddle of tears had swiftly become a great lake of self-hate and pity because those buckets were filled with the tears of the emotionally molested and physically victimized. That lake of tears subsequently became a paralyzed sea as salty and lifeless as the Dead Sea because the tears of all the children of Africa who suffered from war and disease begin to over flow like a waterfall of deceit and betrayal. Then Jurist cried for ten more days and nights because he realized that the buckets of tears that were collected were not from around the world. Those buckets were filled with the tears of the spiritually lost and faithless children within his very own community.

"Jurist, Jurist baby, you okay?" Nandi asked as she softly shakes Jurist by his shoulders. Jurist wakes up and wipes away a tear from his eye.

"Yeah I'm okay. What are you doing here I thought you had to go check on your clients."

"I did," Nandi responds. "I came back because I had forgotten my bucket. I forgot that Ms. Janie grandchildren were over to her home during the week. I always make sure I clean up the bathroom and kitchen after they leave. I heard you cry out so I came to see what was wrong with you. I guess you were having another one of your dreams. Are you sure you okay? I know Ermine's court case must be bothering you."

"No ma, seriously I fine. Now go back to work and don't worry about me."

"Well, just in case I'm going to call Shayla and ask her to stop by and check on you." Nandi grabbed her bucket and walked out the door wearing her white medical jacket, white skirt and white shoes.

Chapter 20
Incarceration

COURT PROCEEDINGS HAVE BEEN GOING ON FOR THE PAST WEEK. The jury has given their decision to the judge. Everyone in the court is waiting and murmuring about what they think the jurors' decision may be. An elderly woman in the back who was a relative of Mr. Putnam utters to one of her kin folk, "I hope they send that no good bastard to jail for the rest of his life. He ain't nothing but a little drug dealing gambler anyway. If he doesn't go to jail now he's going to end up there eventually."

Another, younger woman that lives in the same apartment complex as Ermine's family, whispered to a man in the courtroom, "You should have saw how bad John Putnam beat that boy's mama. How can you blame him? If that had been my son I would have wanted him to do the same thing." Jurist and Nandi were seated behind Mrs. Putnam. Jurist places his hand on Mrs. Putnam's shoulder, leaned over and gave her a hug.

The judge asked for order in the court to get everyone to stifle their comments, "After being judge by a group of his peers, the court finds the defendant Ermine Brown guilty of second degree murder.

The defendant's attorney and the prosecutor has already agreed that although this crime is punishable up to life in prison due to the circumstances and the lack of criminal history of the defendant he is here by ordered to serve twenty-five years with the possibility of early parole after the fifth-tenth year. Mr. Brown will serve his time in a federal prison that will be specified at a later date."

Jurist gazed on in shock at the Judge then at Ermine who had a single tear running down his cheek. In shackles, Ermine is then escorted out of the courtroom by the guard. Ermine stared at his mother who is crying frantically, "No, no not my baby!" Jurist grabbed hold of Mrs. Putnam and told her, "Be strong, be strong. Everything will be all right, everything will be all right."

Chapter 21
Vicious Cycle

JURIST WALKED OUT OF HIS HOME and saw a group of teenage boys carrying machetes and shields preparing to battle. Jurist screamed, "No!" but the gangs continue on as if they couldn't hear him at all. After Jurist realized that the gangs couldn't hear him, he dashed off the porch and ran as fast as he could to reach them before they encountered one another. But no matter how fast Jurist ran he couldn't run fast enough to stop them. They battled almost to the death before troops in white suits showed up at the scene. One of the men in white suits said "freeze" and both the gangs stopped fighting. Soon after a large cage pulled by a team of Clydesdales, galloped towards the gangs and another one of the men in white suits said, "Get in the cage."

The gangs looked at each other then they looked to their leaders and their leaders started walking towards the prisons. Now no more than 30 yards away Jurist screamed, "NO!" as loud as he could with all his heart and the members of both gangs turned their heads in Jurist's direction. Another one of the men in the white suits stepped up to the leaders and said in a soft stern grunt of a tone, "Make them get in right now." The two leaders of the gangs put their machetes to the necks of one of their fellow tribesmen or gang member's neck. Yet still, the other gang members would not move, they just continued to wait for Jurist to reach them.

"Buzz, buzz, buzz," Jurist's alarm goes off and he awakes breathing hard and sweating.

Chapter 22
Graduation

IT'S GRADUATION DAY and proud family members and friends gathered together to give their best wishes to the graduating class. The sun is shining bright although you couldn't tell because the graduation is held inside of the gym. Outside to the right of the gym is the T-shirt man and beside him is the picture woman. They both are trying to make sure that memorabilia of this wonderful occasion is readily available for a reasonable cost. Inside the gym, the guidance counselor has just finished calling everyone across the stage to accept his or her diploma.

"Ladies and Gentlemen let's give a round of applause to the graduating class of 1989." Everyone gave a standing ovation.

"Now we will have words of inspiration from the Senior Class President."

Jurist walked to the microphone, "Good afternoon Principle Green, friends, families, faculty, staff and especially the Class of 1989. I must say my peers and I never thought this day would arrive. Now that it has, it seems as though it has come about rather rapidly, almost too fast. The blindfold of childhood has been removed and we must adjust to the light of a new world. The successes and failures of our past are and will be different from our failures and successes in the future. As young adults we must demand and strive to be the best. We must lift whatever fears lying upon our chest and set them aside. It is now our turn to carry the torch of pride and knowledge. We must do this to keep our sense of community alive and prepare others for the journey across the narrow pathways of life. I have learned a lot and I have gained life-long friends through this educational process and I am sure that my peers feel the same way. However, as we look around we must acknowledge the fact that everyone who started this journey with us is not here with us today. We must try to remember what got us here and not forget the reasons why some of us could not be.

 The line between right and wrong can sometimes be very thin; the ability to see the difference and make the right choice for you is a significant attribute. Now as you set ablaze the roads of success don't forget to bring along your integrity and remember to help those you pass by. On behalf of the graduating class of 1989, I thank you and God Bless us all."

At the end of his speech Jurist envisions Ermine sitting on his bed and locked in his cell. Ermine has his head down and a bible clinched in both his hands.

Chapter 23
College Life

THROUGHOUT SOUTH FLORIDA, there is rich nutritious dirt the color of world before light. However, in Tallahassee there is an abundance of reddish earth that more resembles that of Georgia dirt than Florida soil. This along with other similarities, have led many people to refer to Tallahassee as South Georgia. Many say that the dirt in Tallahassee used to be jet black but the ground begin to change from black to red with the slaughter of the "Red Man." In its virginal days, Tallahassee and much of Florida was primarily inhabited by Native Americans. But as the civilized countries of the world traveled to the West, they eventually came upon Florida and the prostitution of Florida began. The governments of Britain, Spain and U.S were the main pimps fighting for this beautiful child of Mother Nature. Overlooking the original caretakers of this pre-chauvinistic land, the super powers of their time ravished the land with Tallahassee caught in the center of the carnage.

Native American, English, Spanish and African blood, tears and spirits soaked the ground. Some African slave runaways escaped south and formed alliances with the Native American and were for the most part adopted into the Native American community. When the U.S government finally gained custody of Florida, General Andrew Jackson became President, Congress passed the Indian Removal Act and Native Americans were forced to move west to Oklahoma. Some believe that the red dirt is a mark of remembrance left by the souls of Native American that were forced to leave. Now a breeding ground for education and entrepreneurial opportunity, Shayla and Jurist are a new age of Africans seeking tutelage of the spirits of this land.

The last day before the first day of classes, Shayla has awakened early and is currently walking to Jurist's dorm. As Shayla ventures around the exterior of the dorm she noticed a partially open door intentionally left cracked open with a stick. Quietly, Shayla entered and slowly allows the door to close softly so that no one is made aware of her presence. In a stealthy manner, she made her way up the stairs and towards Jurist's floor. She observes that the doors are marked with the names of the students on construction paper taped to the door. Shayla knocked as hard as she could without calling attention to herself. Finally, Jurist's roommate Jason awakes and opened the door.

Softly she whispered, "Oh, I'm sorry to wake you I'm Shayla, Jurist's girlfriend. Can you wake him for me?"

Still yawning and wiping the cold from his eyes. Jason glanced over to Jurist bed and informs her of Jurist absence.

Puzzled, she asked, "Do you know where he went?"

"I didn't even know he was gone." Jason stretches and asked Shayla for the time.

"Seven-Thirty" she told him.

Jason walked away from the door and said to Shayla, "I'm about to go back to bed. You're welcome to come in and wait but if the RA comes by I do know how you got in here."

"Thanks but I think I should go. When Jurist returns, I would appreciate it if you would tell him that I stopped by."

Already lying in the bed with his head on the pillow Jason said, "Sure." Shayla closed the door and made her escape out of the dorm. But as she walked down the stairs and approaches the door. It opened and Jurist exploded through it. Jurist looked up in surprise and shouted, "Shayla!"

"Jurist!" Shayla responds in shock.

"What are you doing here," he asked?

"I stopped by to see you and while walking by the dorm I noticed that this door was open."

"Yeah, I cracked it open because I didn't want to have to walk all the way around to the front to get in when I got back."

Intrigued about where Jurist could have gone this early in the morning Shayla asked, "So, where have you been?"

Jurist walked and guides Shayla out of the dorm, "I couldn't sleep so I took a walk around campus. What made you walk all the way over here?"

"I couldn't sleep either and I kept thinking about you."

A smile rushed over Jurist face. Jurist looked at Shayla and stared at her from head to toe. His initial thought was that Shayla was oddly dressed so early in the morning but she looked so beautiful that he could do nothing but compliment her.

"That's a beautiful dress you're wearing."

"Why thank you," she said as she blushed and walked closer to Jurist. "I put it on because I thought you would like it." Shayla's sundress was vibrantly colored with flower-patterns that rivaled the most beautiful garden. It manipulated the colors of a chrysanthemum and purple rose and combined them in a perfect design. "I thought that it would be great if we could spend the last day before class together. I wanted us to be us before things become so hectic."

"That's a great idea. Damn it!"

"What is it?"

"I was intending to walk to the post office. I'm waiting on some important mail."

"Well come on, we can walk their together."

Jurist and Shayla arrive at the post office. Jurist walked over to his mailbox and opened it. Inside it there are two envelopes one is a credit card application and the other is a letter from Ermine. Jurist throws the credit card application in the garbage and hesitates before opening the letter from Ermine. Jurist walked away from his box and turned his back towards Shayla.

"Baby, give me a minute."

"Go ahead baby, I'm going to go and check my box. I'll wait for you by the exit."

Jurist unfolded the note and began to read.

"What's up college boy? I was happy to see you in the courtroom. I appreciate you being by my mama's side. Hey don't feel bad about what happened at the crib there was nothing you could have done to stop it. Besides I would feel terrible if you were in here with me, instead of being in college with Shayla. You know how we used to hear all those stories about prison, take it from me they're true. Man, they're a lot of blacks in here. But it's real separated. I mean way more than on the streets. I don't know what to do. Most of the white guys in here are just racist pigs and all the brothers think I'm just a black wanna be. The best thing is that I see a couple familiar faces. You remember John-John off 3rd street and Goony off 10th they're in here to. They tell me little things about this joint to help me keep my nose clean, but back to you. Make sure you learn as much as you can and don't forget that there's a little hustle in everything we do including college. I've also done some calculating and my calculations tell me that you'll be a big time lawyer before I get out of here. Just promise me that when you become a big timer you'll take over my case. I have faith in you.

Stay strong. Ermine.

P.S tell Shayla I said hello and to get one of those college chicks to write me and send me some pictures.

Jurist took a moment to clear his throat and wipe away the lone tear that escaped his right eye. As Jurist walked back to Shayla she can sense the change in Jurist's persona.

"Baby is everything all right?"

"Yeah, everything's fine baby, everything's cool."

Chapter 24
The Legend Begins

TWO YEARS HAVE PASSED BY and Jurist is a junior with an outstanding record in both the college and local community. Around campus they call him little Thurgood, it all started after Jurist helped this one girl who was trying to get in a sorority but she did not have enough money to pledge. Somehow Jurist helped the girl get an emergency loan from the school that allowed her to pledge that semester. Ever since that incident occurred any time someone on campus that knew of Jurist had a problem with housing, grades or financial aid they ran to Jurist so he could help them find a solution. But Jurist didn't begin cultivating his community action involvement until he ran into Amos one evening. Amos was on his way to a Black Action Movement meeting. Jurist had heard about the group around campus but he had never followed through to gain additional information. But as luck would have it he saw Amos one evening as he was about to attend a meeting. So Amos invited him. Jurist was immediately enthralled and signed up for membership. Saul Jefferies was the president and he was one of those people who set high goals and expected production from every member. Jurist respected his leadership ability and management skills. At the time there were only 15 members of BAM. But Jurist would soon change that. Jurist and Saul never worked directly together nonetheless Saul noticed that Jurist was an effective and tenacious worker. Therefore, Saul would make Jurist an assistant in a lot of field expeditions such as gathering research information from both the students and residents around the community. Jurist liked it because it gave him the opportunity to meet new people and really get a since of the problems that affected the neighborhoods. Jurist would sit and talk with a lot of different people throughout the community and learn about the challenges they faced. Jurist quickly came to the revelation that the most prevalent problem affecting the majority of the neighborhoods was economic instability and the lack of family cohesiveness. Moreover, Jurist had this magical skill that allowed him to get personal information from even the most down trodden individuals. He had a sincere and likeable personality which resonated with almost everyone he encountered. People around the community began thinking that Jurist was president of the organization. Soon his reputation for being a good, smart, hard-working young man began to spread.

Presently, he is at a BAM quarterly review meeting giving one of his signature speeches.

"Malcolm X once said, 'Our people have made the mistake of confusing the methods with the objectives. As long as we agree on objectives, we should never fall out with each other just because we believe in different methods or tactics or strategy. We have to keep in mind at all times that we are not fighting for separation. We are fighting for recognition as free humans in this society.' With this premise in mind, I believe it's time for us to extend the hand of brother and sisterhood to other black groups and individuals. We must stop merely gathering data to talk about what we need in the black communities. We have to start implementing programs within these communities. After the people start to see that we're not just talking, I promise you membership will flourish and people will follow. Even members of other organizations will lend helping hands. Our aim must be to make alliances and let the people decide who they want to represent them. This project should be named the

Forth-Right Commission and I move that this commission be accepted and started immediately under my leadership but if and only if nobody is in disagreement."

Shayla standing near Jurist quickly raised her hand and said, "I second that motion."

Saul Jefferies, the president of BAM, recognized that a motion had been made and properly seconded. And although he had some reservations about the program, as president, this is a process in which he has very limited power. Furthermore, he did not want to look as if he went against the will of the people should they be of the same mind as Jurist. "All those who agree say ye." Everyone at the meeting said ye and it was heard like a wave crossing the ocean. "All those who oppose say nay." Total silence submerged the room. "Are there any that abstain?" The silence continued. "Then by unanimous decision, The Forth-Right Commission will start immediately under the leadership of Jurist Johnson." Saul shakes Jurist hand, smiled at him, and told him congratulations.

"Thank you, Saul," Jurist humbly responds.

As Jurist took his seat, Shayla leaned over, and whispered in Jurist's right ear.

"This is great Jurist. You finally have leadership over your own committee. I'm so proud of you."

Jurist whispered back, "Don't be so proud of me just yet we still have a lot of work ahead of us. Here take these sign-up sheets, and see how many members we can get to help us with getting this commission rolling."

Chapter 25
The Report

PROFESSOR CONAN AND THE REST OF THE SUPREME COUNCIL, on behalf of the New Futures Association, were on a conference call with each other discussing Jurist progress. Professor Conan is providing the other executive members a synopsis of what has been transpiring at the BAM.

"I have good news ladies and gentlemen it seems as though our caterpillar have started to weave his cocoon. He has his own leadership committee to bring in new membership from other groups. After his no doubt success with this commission, he will soon be voted into presidency with the help of his new members. But his taste for leadership won't stop there. No, no our little Jurist will surely challenge for a position within the New Future Association where he will naturally take his rightful position right here amongst us. Jamal, I want your company to contribute a nice lump sum to the chapter as soon as Jurist becomes president."

"Economic stability is always helpful."

Jamal responds, "Omar, what makes you so sure of Jurist and his capability to lead?"

"Because, it's his birth right."

Meanwhile, Jurist and the Forth-Right Commission are working hard making flyers, pamphlets and banners. They are also exchanging ideas. Damon, a volunteer with the Forth-Right Commission, called out to Jurist. "Jurist the flyers are almost through printing."

"Well, as soon as they are finished give everyone in the committee a hundred flyers each. Remind them that they are to put them up in the pre-designated locations. Damon you are in charge of making sure there is no church, school, bus-station or recreation center without some sort of BAM information readily available. Now does anyone have any ideas they want to voice."

Isis, the vibrant young sister that Jurist met when he and Shayla first traveled to Tallahassee has also volunteered to help Jurist. She quickly answered, "Yes, I have an idea Jurist."

Shayla turned and look at Isis with a wary eye.

"Why don't we have a joint seminar were representatives from each group is on the panel to discuss issues concerning the disadvantaged communities."

Shayla interjects, "I thought this wasn't supposed to be a competition."

Isis retorts, "It's not a competition, it's a forum where everyone has an opportunity to fine-tune the ideas of others to bring about change."

"That's a great idea Isis," said Jurist. "Isis you're responsible for making this forum happen. Moreover, you will decide what issues will be discussed. But please no more than 2 issues. I was also thinking about making pamphlets for people to read, and learn

about BAM's beliefs and views. Shayla I would appreciate it if you
would head this committee."

"No problem but I need someone to help me gather information."

To Shayla's surprise, Isis volunteers to help her.

Jurist smiled delighted at the notion that maybe if Shayla and Isis
can complete this job together they will develop a better
relationship with one another. "That's great. I'm sure you ladies
will have it done in no time."

The next day Isis and Shayla met up at the campus-copying center
to finish the pamphlets. Shayla on schedule as usual has started
working already. Every minute that passed, she became more and
more upset with Isis. Sixteen minutes have passed by, and
suddenly Isis walked in.

"Hi Shayla sorry I'm late, I had to run a copy of the discussions for
the forum over to Jurist to get his take on them."

"You could have just given it to me and I would have made sure he
got them when he comes over later."

"Like I said I'm sorry. Now what do you need my help with?"

Tired of hiding her discontent and distrust of Isis, Shayla reacts and
lashes out with her initial thoughts.

"You must have lost your mind if you think I can't see straight
through these little games you're playing. Well, trying to play."
Isis confused by Shayla's remarks snaps back, "Girl, I don't have the
slightest idea what you're talking about."

Shayla steps closer to Isis, "Well let me break it down for you then.
Stop trying to holla at my man."

Un-intimidated but recognizing that Shayla is really upset, Isis leisurely replies, "Feeling a little insecure are we? Look **sistah**, I'm not going to sit here and lie to you. I think Jurist is one of the most stimulating men I've ever seen. But I respect the bond that you and Jurist share. I would consider myself less than a **sistah** if I tried to break ya'll bond. However, if my sexuality scares you maybe you need to spend less time thinking about me and Jurist and more time with him. Or is his work more important than you? Now that we have that issue out of the way, I would really like to hurry up and finish these pamphlets.

Shayla stared at Isis vehemently "Say what you want, but stay away from my man. And I mean that."

Realizing that she may have done more harm than good Isis calms down the tone of her rhetoric. "Look I'm sorry for what I said. Truthfully, I volunteered to help you with this project because I believe in what Jurist and the rest of the organization's member are trying to do. I am your sister I am not your enemy. So please accept my friendship while it's still on the table because you really do not want me as an enemy. I use to have a lot of respect for you. I thought to myself, if Jurist chose her to be his girl she must have some very admiral attributes. But I never would have thought that jealousy would be the characteristic that controlled you." Isis walked out the door and leaves Shayla pondering her actions and remarks.

Chapter 26
Clarity

JURIST IS IN HIS ROOM READING THE NEW NEGRO BY ARTHUR SCHOMBERG when the phone rang. Jurist answered the phone, and is shocked to find out that it was Professor Conan who called him. They hold casual conversation in the beginning. Then the Professor advises Jurist that he wants to meet with him as soon as possible. Jurist told the Professor that he could meet him at his office in 20 minutes. As Jurist gathered his things, he contemplates why the Professor would call him to setup a meeting in such short time. Jurist entered the Professor's office, and made small talk with the receptionist. The receptionist advises the Professor of Jurist arrival, and told Jurist to walk on through to the office chamber. Professor Conan, already standing, walked up to Jurist to shake his hand. Jurist noticed the level of respect it signifies for the Professor to walk over to him, and shake his hand as he entered the room. "Jurist, I'm glad you came on such short notice."

"There isn't a problem or anything is it Professor?"

"No, no there's nothing wrong. Here have a seat."

"How is Mrs. Conan doing?"

"She is doing well; she is attending a conference in Alabama." I need to go to my house to grab a couple of things you don't mind riding with me do you?"

"No sir, I don't mind at all."

As they walk to the car, and ride to Professor's Conan home, Professor Conan began to share more information about why he wanted to meet with Jurist.

"Jurist, I made a list of the classes that will allow you to complete your undergraduate course requirements, and prepare you for law school."

"Thanks Professor I appreciate it."

Before long they arrive at the Professor's home. "You and your wife really have a beautiful home. When Shayla and I get married I want to get her a house just like this one."

"You and Shayla are very close. That's good. A good woman keeps a man focused however they tend to need a lot of attention themselves. Especially when their boyfriend is in the spotlight as much as you are. Come follow me to my study. Do you remember the first conversation we had in this room?"

"Yes. I do. We talked about True Freedom."

"Yes, and although African-Americans as a people have made great strides since the days of legalized slavery; our people still have not gained true freedom."

"But we are free to choose to do anything a white man can do."

"Yeah, we're free. Free to join their military, run their businesses, and fix their machinery. But do we have the freedom not to participate. Do we have freedom not to thirst for money? Do we have freedom to rehabilitate our own instead of imprisoning them? Well Professor, do we?"

"Each person lives their life the way they choose to live it."

"Do they? Well tell me from your limited view of the world how do you perceive it?"

"Hypothetically speaking, look at the Earth as it is, our mother, a mother that reared two children, one named man, and the other named animal, animal being the older of the two. Although the mother provides man, and animal everything they need to survive without prejudice, man chooses to separate himself from both his mother and his brother returning only to steal, kidnap, and plunder to prove his dominance over both his brother and mother. That's how I see the world."

"That was a very bleak illustration of man's contribution to the world, and you have holes in your analogy. Where's the father, and what's his role? Secondly, how do you account for the civilizations that have, and still do coexist within the balance of nature? The classes that are on that list will teach you how to plug those holes, and help you hypothesize a more noteworthy theory."

"Professor Conan I can't tell you how much I appreciate you helping me, and if there's anything I can do to return the favor just let me know, and it's done. But I hope you don't get offended by what I'm about to say. Sometimes I get the feeling as if you have some type of hidden agenda. Nonetheless, I just want you to know that whatever you want of me I am here to give it.

"Actually there is one thing. But it's not just for me."

"What is it?"

"Jurist there is something very important I want to share with you but the only way I can tell you, is if you swear to keep this secret with your life. For what I am about to tell you is the most important

138

secret that our people have kept since Underground Railroad."
Jurist looked Professor Conan directly in his eyes, and said "I
swear".

"With your life?"

"With my life Sir."

Alright but know this from this day forth your life will never be the
same.

"First let me explain to you the true nature, and purpose of The
New Future Association. You see New Future was actually founded
in 1963 by a group of business men who had wealth, power, and
influence not just within the black community but in other ethnic
societies as well. Their goal was to find the next messiah or leader
for our nation."

"Why couldn't one of them be the leader?"

"Their positions in life would not allow them to actively partake in
such a revolutionary position but their contributions, and ability to
network across the nation have helped greatly. Today, NFA helps to
sponsor hundreds of organizations across the globe, and all of these
organizations will soon be under the supervision of one particular
person to help develop a nation autonomous from the sustained
government, a nation for black people created by black people. You
see Jurist, black people can't continue to wait for these programs
developed by researchers of the majority to heal our communities;
this is a task we must undertake to guarantee the survival of our
people not only here but aboard. Your father believed in the
purpose and principles of the NFA. As a matter of fact, he was a
recruiter for the very same position that will be offered to you."

Jurist got up from his seat, and started to pace around the room.
"I can't believe what I'm hearing. You knew my father. How did
you get to know my father? You must have the wrong person."

"You don't have to listen to me, here listen to your father."
Professor Conan grabbed a tape out his drawer, and places it in a
tape recorder in front of Jurist.

"Go ahead, press play."

Jurist pulled the recorder closer, and press the play button. First
there is static then all of a sudden a voice is heard.

"How long, how long will we wait? How long will our people
continue to be the kings and queens of sorrow for this Nation? We
are dying. Do you hear me? We are dying because we cannot live
the lives we were put here to live. Suppressed we are, dependent we
are, crippled we are, groomed we are, defeated we are not. Decades,
centuries, and millenniums have passed, and we are still at war with
the menace of the years. But as long as we have the ability to
procreate we will continue to have soldiers willing to fight. God just
blessed me with a son, his name is Jurist (meaning one
knowledgeable of the law), and when I am no longer here to
continue the fight, he will take his rightful position amongst the
great warriors of his time ready to battle for the good of his people."
Conan stopped the tape.

"Do you believe me now?"

"I don't get it, why my mother never told me any of this."

"Jurist your mother had already lost a husband to the struggle you
think she was going to risk losing you, her only son as well. But you
are a man now, able to make decisions for yourself. I'm only
offering you your birth right, the right to lead the revolution as a
good soldier of God."

The telephone rang.

"I'll give you a couple of days to think about it."

"Go ahead, and take your call. I'm going to take a walk."

"Jurist, if you want to know anything about your father just ask me. If you don't agree with the answer I provide you, look in a mirror, gaze through your eyes, and there you will find the answer you seek."

Chapter 27
The Report II

YEARS HAVE PASSED SINCE PROFESSOR CONAN HAD HIS TALK WITH JURIST. Patiently awaiting the arrival of a dear friend the reflection of Professor Conan can be seen in the window of the airport waiting area. He's wearing a white-collar button up shirt with gold couplings, black pin-striped vest with pants to match, and African leather shoes. Clean from head to toe similar to a Wall Street tycoon. After de-boarding the plane Mr. Sharrieff walked towards Professor Conan, and taps his right shoulder with his right hand. Professor Conan stood as Mr. Sharrieff greets him by shaking his hand, and saying, "It's good to see you old man."

"It's good to see you as well my friend."

"So, how is our recruit handling his new found responsibility? Is he along for the ride?"

"Not only is he handling things, he's excelled, and at a more rapid pace than we originally anticipated."

"Have you explained everything to him?"

"Everything he needs to know for right now."

"And he's in total agreement with what we're asking of him."

"I think this may answer all of your questions?" He hands Mr. Sharrieff a folder with documents inside.

"What's this?"

"It's a report of Jurist's progress." Mr. Sharrieff skims through the report.

"Are all these numbers correct?"

"Yep!" Professor Conan proudly responds.

"Shayla told me that you all were busy but this is astonishing. Membership has flourished by 300 percent plus the addition of volunteer tutorial service, and parent-child community involvement groups. I see that they have established several Community Learning Centers across the region, and that's a extremely large budget increase. Do you think anybody suspect's New Future's involvement with BAM?"

"Sshh! Professor Conan make sure that Mr. Sharrieff understands that New Future is not to be mentioned. Nobody outside the council is aware."

"So it seems that I was right about Jurist being the one."

"Yes it does. Yes it does. At first I was worried that the Council may think that I was trying to pull some lineage type move, but they embraced him quicker than I did."

"Graduation is coming up soon. Where is he going to attend law school?"

"The best place for BAM to expand, and gain widespread attention is Washington, DC. Therefore, we decided that H.U. would be the best choice."

"Does this mean that the council is in full agreement with Jurist's eventual position?"

"Let's just say that everything is tranquil amongst the council."

Chapter 28
Ermine's Letter

JURIST IS AT HIS APARTMENT OPENING HIS MAIL, and he noticed that he has received another letter from Ermine. He sat on his couch, and put the other mail on the coffee table. As he began to read he imagined Ermine sitting in his cell.

Ermines Letter:

What's up militant black man? I hope you're up there letting them know that we aren't all evil little white men born to hate black men while chasing black woman. Because you know I ain't with that hate the black men shit, although I will chase a couple sisters though, but hey who wouldn't. But for real thanks for the books you sent me they were really deep. They give me a little insight as to what's going on in the streets. I guess you can say that were screwed ha. It's funny how when we were in school they never taught us any of this stuff. Now I'm beginning to see why white people have this unhidden distrust for one another, and black people. It's all about the money. If you have it you acquire status, and respect but if you're a have not you're punished for not having. Shit, the way I see it. Ya'll got it bad because ya'll, and the

Indians too, are their conscience; forever reminding them of their most beastly behavior and past. Kind of like how my mother would always get mad at me, and tell me how I remind her of my father. I know I'm not going to comprehend everything but at least I have you to help teach me. But it would be good if you could come visit ya boy every now and then. I appreciate the books, and letters, but it would mean a lot to me if you came to see a nigga, I mean a brother. Damn, it's hard to believe that four years have gone by so fast. I only have twenty-one years left. My mom is moving to Georgia with my Aunt Tina. When she leaves the guys in here will really be my closest family. I talk about you with the guys all the time. I told them about your movement, and some of them say that when they get out they're going to join. I even let them read some of the books you send. Who knows, maybe I'll be able to start a BAM chapter in here someday. Well, I'll see you later.

Your boy forever, Ermine.

Jurist thinks to himself, "That's a great idea. Develop a plan for brothers and sisters who are institutionalized within the prison system to join BAM, but how? I need to schedule a meeting with Professor Conan." Jurist picked up the phone to call Professor Conan but no one answered so he has to leave a message. He then immediately started typing his proposal for a Reclamation program for prison inmates. A few minutes pass there is a knock at his door. Jurist walked over to the door, opened it, and saw that it is Shayla.

"Hey baby, I brought you some lunch."

"Thanks. What is it? It smells great. My friend Sonja cooked some curry chicken and rice. Baby, you are the greatest!"

"I know. What were you working on?"

"I'm drafting a proposal for this idea I got after reading a letter I received from Ermine. You want to proofread it when I'm finished?"

"Sure, how is E doing?"

"He said he's doing well, but he wants me to come visit him."

"After graduation let's schedule a trip to see him."

"If things go the way I want them to, I'm going to take a trip there in two weeks."

"But graduation is only a month away."

"Exactly, I want to have this done before graduation."

"I can't just get up, and leave to go to West Palm Beach on such short notice."

"No problem, I'll just ask someone else to fly down with me."

"Who Isis? I'm sure you'll love to take her with you wouldn't you."

"Come on now. Stop acting so jealous, and come read this." Jurist hands Shayla the proposal. "I don't feel like reading it right now," she said with a pinch of attitude. "You like her don't you?"

"Who Isis? Yeah, of course I like her. She's a nice girl. But that don't mean I want to be with her." Jurist, stood up, and walk towards Shayla. "Baby, listen to me. "I love you." Jurist grabbed Shayla by her waist, and pulled her closer to him. "I always have, and I always will. You know you're the only woman for me."

Shayla's lack luster attempts to push Jurist away fails as she knew they would. With sincerity in her eyes she said, "Yeah, I know you love me but sometimes I feel that you forget, and I know that there are dozens of women just like Isis who want to be with you. And I know that you know that she wants to take my place."

Jurist grabbed Shayla tighter, "I don't know about all that but come here." Jurist grabbed Shayla's hand, and leads her to his room. "Let me show you what I do know."

Chapter 29
Community Pacemaker

ON HIS WAY TO MEET WITH PROFESSOR CONAN, Jurist re-read his proposal, and cross exams it to prepare himself for the many questions that he is sure Professor Conan will bombard him with. He thinks to himself, "I have barely earned one chevron, and here I am trying to propose such a bold idea. I must be crazy." But then he thinks about the tremendous amount of good this program can accomplish if executed effectively. Memories of childhood friends, and neighbors flood his mind. Images of young men getting out of jails and prisons with no hope standing on street corners killing themselves, and hurting their community just for the chance to exist another day. In this concrete jungle, going to prison is the equivalent of losing a leg while living in the bushes of Africa. Jurist envisions his program as a prosthetic leg for the prison community.

"Jurist, I must admit that it's a very interesting proposal. But it's going to be hard to pull off."

"I know but it will be worth it."

"Let me make sure I understand this correctly. You want BAM to establish a program that teaches prisoners comprehensive skills, job readiness, family structure, and program management. Furthermore, this program is to extend into the homes of these prisoners to teach their families these skills as well." Jurist can hear the hint of disbelief in Professor Conan's voice.

"Correct."

"What about funding? Not to mention the hundreds of man hours, and therapeutic counseling that will be needed?"

"We can try to get the program funded as a nonprofit organization, and pay some of those who work for the program."

"Wait, wait, wait, before you go to the government. Let me talk to the Council, and get the initial funding. Then after we gain a little success with the program, and gain additional funding from other private agencies outside the council then you can go to the government for help."

"So we're in business." Jurist gave that million dollar smile of his, and gave Professor Conan a hug. This is great! Trust me I will not let you down."

"Well, I still have to run it by the Council but you do have my vote. Besides you haven't failed me yet."

"Thanks Professor, I knew you wouldn't let me down." Jurist grabbed his things, and started to bolt towards the door.

"Where are you in such a rush to go?"

"I have to go catch a flight to West Palm Beach. I have some family matters to take care of, and my mother is expecting me."

"Godspeed, and tell your mother I send my greetings."

Jurist arrives at the West Palm Beach airport, and Nandi is near the luggage area waiting for his plane to un-board. When Nandi saw Jurist she does what every mother does. She gave him a big hug, and asked him a million questions about how he is doing. And then she got to her main question.

"Now what's so important you had to come to Palm Beach a week before your graduation? Are you sure everything is alright?"
Jurist responds to her with one name "Ermine!"
Stunned by Jurist's reply she repeats him, "Ermine. What's wrong with Ermine?"

"Nothing ma, I'll explain it to you on the way to the jailhouse."

Chapter 30
Mental Graveyard

*I see myself running through the forest of inner health. Adoration,
affection, and tenderness elude me seemingly eternally.
Perpetually, I hear pain, touch death, taste hurt, and smell fear all
around me. I pass a village surrounded by a fire of disarray with
kids infinitely challenging & daring each other to jump into the
fiery wall of deceit. I heard one kid say, "He's crazy, he'll do it."
Instantaneously, I saw my childlike self amongst the encased
village children with their intrigued eyes watching my every step.
Each one of them screamed for help. So, I took the leap. They
consistently asked me to show them my heart, but I couldn't. For I
was the evolution of petty heartfelt emotions, logics guided my
every course of action. Never could I remember longing for
earned love like I did on that day. I saw no darlingness within my
world therefore loving emotions were obsolete in my mind. When
one of the children asked me why the fire didn't burn me, I could
not answer him. For no logic could explain why my skin had not
been unrecognizably scorched. Alien to my newfound
environment I set out to explore the uncommon realm. As I turned
my back to the crowd of juveniles, one starts to chant, "Show us
your heart." I continued to walk as if I could not hear her, then the*

others started to chant. "Show us your heart, show us your heart,"
I replied, "I know nothing of this heart you speak of." One boy
throws a pair of doves towards me, "Here, here, here is love catch
it," but the doves flew far over my head. In that instance I lost my
first chance for love. Another girl blew a kiss at me but I could not
see where it had fallen; love had escaped my grasp once again.
Suddenly, I heard a mother's voice calling, and all the kids
disappeared. A faint sound of laughter penetrated my ears from
my most southern side. Unfamiliar faces clouded my vision,
tension slowly coursed through my veins. While blood dripped
from my fingers, fear rushed me like a rhino. What was
happening to me? Am I condemned to die in this heavenly garden
of prosperity? Hazily, I hear a voice asked me once again, "Where
is your heart?" Suddenly, I begin to ask myself. Where is my
heart?

ENTERING THE PRISON PRESENTED TROUBLING FEELINGS FOR JURIST. As soon as he walked in the complex, he stepped through a metal detector, and to a desk in which the guard took his ID, and asked who he's there to visit. Jurist in a transit motion surveys the room, glancing over everything from the green pasty looking walls to the half a dozen unhidden cameras. The guard told Jurist how to get to the area to meet Ermine. Jurist walked through the prison listening in on every conversation, as he made his way toward the visiting area. Once he maked it to the next level, Jurist is identified, and the guard confirmed who he was there to meet. He hears a guard summon Ermine over the intercom telling him to report to the visitor's station. This whole experience felt surreal to Jurist as he sat in front of the glass window awaiting Ermine. But when Ermine finally walked through the door, and looked at him a huge smile erupted on both their faces as they picked up the phone to talk to one another.

"Damn man, I hardly recognized you. What, what you doing here?"

"Your idea in your letter."

"What idea?"

"Your idea about creating a BAM chapter in here."
"Man, you got to be kidding me. I haven't seen you in four years, and now you've finally come to see me, you want to talk to me about starting a prison chapter for your club."

"It's not like that E you know we run way deeper that man. The truth of the matter is that I really didn't want to see you like this. Caged like some animal."

"I can't lie man, I thought you had forgot about your boy for a minute."

"Nall man, I could never do that."

"So what you got cooking in that dome of yours."

"I talked to my people about the possibility of a chapter down here, and although it will be a hard task we all feel it can be done. We are in the process of writing a grant to get the government to fund the program in a year or so."

"What is the program going to be set up to do?"

"It will function as a tool utilized by BAM members to teach, counsel, and mediate prisoners and their families."

"Teach and counsel us, shit ya'll going to be the ones needing the counseling. Man, that letter, that letter was just wishful thinking. It's a totally different world in here. There is no rehabilitation for most of the guys in here."

"The world in here, and out there are the same, it's just that the world in here is much closer to reality, therefore more visible."

"So, how are you going to make this work?"

"You mean, how are we going to make this work?" Jurist stared at

Ermine with conviction in his eyes, and Ermine grins at him. "The hardest part is going to be convincing brothers to enlist in the program. That's where you come in."

"Jurist if you haven't noticed I'm still white."

"That's why it's going to work, you are the exception to the rules, the glitch in the matrix so to speak. I gave the warden a complete overview of our program objectives and goals to give to you. I'll be back after graduation to speak to the rest of the prisoners to try to get them to apply for acceptance into the program. But while I'm gone I need you to be my mouth piece."

"Bruh, I got you covered."

"I have never doubted that."

"Enough with all that business talk. How you doing?"

"I told you man everything's going to be ok."

"No, No I mean with you. How are you doing? And what's taking you and Shayla so long?"

"So long to do what?"

"To get married make a little Jurist."

"We're waiting for the right time."

I appreciate the fact that you want me to partake in the wedding festivities, but J, I got at least eleven more years until I am eligible for parole, and I don't think Shayla is trying to wait that long. Besides that, if I've learned anything living in here; I've learned that the right time is anytime you can make it happen."

"I know I know."

"Plus, I've known you and Shayla longer than anyone. Shayla is the one for you."

"I know that too."

"Well act like you know, and let her know. Living in here for the last half decade gave me a lot of time to think and reflect back on things that are important to me. The one thing that I lacked most is love. Love is the only thing that keeps most of us going, and in here it's more precious than gold."

"Damn man, this is all my fault, if I..." Ermine interrupts Jurist.

"Hey man, don't worry. Like I said it was me. Now hurry up, and become a big time lawyer, and get me out of here, before Shayla's clock started ticking."

"I love you E"

"I love you to bruh."

"Hey Jurist,"

"Yeah bruh, what's up?"

"Next time you come visit at least bring a sister with you."

"Okay, I got you."

"A fine one!" Ermine shouted, and smiled as he mimics his hands in the shape of a woman.

Chapter 31
Miscommunication

JURIST REALLY TOOK ERMINES ADVICE ABOUT SHAYLA TO HEART. So as soon as he landed he called Isis, and asked her to help him complete some work at the office so he could spend some extra time alone with Shayla.

"Isis I appreciate you helping with these files on such short notice. Now I'll be able to surprise Shayla, and we'll finally be able to get to spend some real time together."

"No problem bruh, besides you, and ol' girl need to spend some time alone. I'll be right back. I need to go to the ladies room."
As Isis leaves the room to go to the restroom Shayla walked through the front door and saw Jurist.

"Jurist! Why didn't you tell me you me you were catching an earlier flight back?"

"What's up baby? I was trying to surprise you."

"Well you did. How did things go with Ermine?"

"Everything went well."

"You know I will do my best to help you, but are you sure this goal of yours is attainable, to be honest I'm not sure if I'm comfortable with the entire situation. Baby you got to admit it, most of these men are in jail for good reasons even Ermine. He did kill his own father."

"Come on baby you know as well as I do that most of those men and women deserve rehabilitation not imprisonment in a Slav eristic institution where they wait to be sold to the highest bidder. Shayla, you and I, we are the new aged abolitionist. This is our chosen way of life."

Shayla hears the water running in the bathroom. "What's that? Is someone else here?"

"Yeah, that's Isis she came over to help me finish filing some things away so I could hurry up, and get to you."

"Oh yeah. You see Jurist this is exactly what I'm talking about." Isis hears Shayla and Jurist arguing so she stood around the corner, and listened to them.

"Come on Shayla don't start with this now, Isis came over to help me just so I would be able to spend more time with you."

"Why is it always so convenient for you to call Isis when you need help?"

"She's always willing to help."

"I wonder why Jurist, why is she always so willing to help?"

"Because she believes that BAM is doing that right thing."

"Are you sure you aren't the reason why she's so dedicated? I don't see her breaking her neck to help nobody else within the organization but every time Jurist needs some help she's always willing to give an extra hand."

"Shayla I really don't need this right now. There is a lot of work to get done. The deadline for the warden's policy is in one month, and we haven't even finished the first draft. So can we finish this conversation at a later date?"

Isis walked in. "Isis can you pick up the graphs and charts from the copy center for me please."

Shayla infuriated about the entire situation spitefully volunteers,

"No, don't worry about it Isis, I'll go pick them up; I was on my way out anyway." Shayla rushed out the door.

Chapter 32
Graduation Party

ON THE OTHER SIDE OF TOWN, a group of students are throwing a party. There were guys and girls running around having a good time playing, laughing, and flirting. Although the party is mildly diversified, most of the people there were Caucasian. Inside the house there were some people taking shots, and chugging beer, and even though some of the guys were at least twenty-one years old, most of the girls were around nineteen years of age.

Nevertheless, majority of the young ladies were drinking as well. Dale, a good looking nursing student, who is preparing to graduate next semester, was partying at the house as well. After partaking in the shot contest he started conversing with two beautiful sophomores Jennifer and Sandy. Dale noticed the girls laughing at him as he left the shot table, and stumbled over a couple people. So he introduced himself, and told some jokes that made the already inebriated girls laugh even harder. Although he is drunk, Dale senses the strong potential to coach the girls into a possible sexual encounter.

"So where do you all live," he said in a slow drowsy voice?

"We have an apartment a couple blocks down the road."

"Well how about we go and grab something to eat, and then go back to ya'll place for an after party. That way we don't have to do so much yelling to talk to each other. You see the guy over there."

Dale points at this guy that looked like the typical volleyball player, "That's my best friend and roommate."

Dale called Bobby over to even the odds. Because of the loud music he screamed, "Hey, Hey Bobby, come here." Bobby is a very well endowed musician, who the girls have seen around campus. "This is Jennifer and Sandy, we are about to ditch this place to get something to eat, and go back to their place for an after party, you in?"

"Of course I'm in," Bobby responds in an exuberant fashion. You know me buddy I'm never one to miss a good party; as long as I don't have to drive." Bobby whispered, "If you all haven't noticed, I'm a little bit tipsy." The girls laugh and giggle. "Don't worry Bobby I'll drive," said Jennifer. Dale intercedes, "No, No, No, I'll drive. All of you have been drinking, and I'm the oldest. Besides I'll be a nurse in a few months, I know how much I can drink."

Everyone nod in agreement, and said 'Okay,' then walked to the car. So they walk over to Dale's black mustang, and the girls quickly start to admire it. As they get in Sandy caresses the leather seats like a pair of Prada shoes. Before they can get moving Sandy asked Dale to play a song from Guns and Roses. Jennifer then interjects, "No, put in Nirvana, I love Nirvana," she said in a sexy tone as she rubs Dale's leg. Needless to say, Dale put in a Nirvana tape, and speeds out of the parking lot. "Yeah," you hear Bobby scream as Jennifer turned the music louder. Then both the girls start to howl and scream.

Meanwhile, Shayla has picked up the graphs from the copy center, and is sitting at a red light upset and depressed. As she sat she began to ponder, "How could he do something like that to me. He knows that I don't trust that girl, yet still he continues to disregard my feelings. For what? What would make him think it's alright to call her before calling me, and at least let me know he was safe. Would he really cheat on me with her? Part of me wants to believe him but my woman's intuition is telling me something isn't right with their relationship. It has to be something going on, but how do I not trust him when he has never given me a reason not to trust him before. This is all Isis fault. I have told her too many times to stop trying to get so close to Jurist. I swear if that girl had just said one more thing to me, it would have been on. As a matter of fact, I wish she would have said something to me so I could have shown her not to keep getting in the way of what I'm feeling. Listen to me, I'm tripping. Lord help me. Shayla began to pray.

At this point, the mustang is now traveling at about 65 mph, and approaching the light where Shayla is waiting. When Shayla's light turned green, she opened her eyes, lifts her head from praying, and accelerated without looking to either side. As soon as Shayla reached the intersection, she is struck on the driver's side by Dale's mustang.

Back at the office Jurist and Isis are talking. "Jurist I know it's none of my business but you handled that situation all wrong my brother. Shayla's feeling a little insecure right now, all she wants is a little affection and attention from you."

Still upset about the incident, and disappointed that Shayla does not trust him. Jurist replies, "I appreciate the advice, but you're right Isis, this is none of your business. If she comes back here tell her I said to meet me at my place."

When Jurist made it to his apartment, and he noticed that his message light is flickering so he began to check his messages. A computerized voice began, "You have three un-played messages. Your first un-played message, "Jurist this is Professor Conan I hope you made it in safely if I know you you're probably at the office. But give me a call when you receive this message." Computerized voice,

"Message deleted. Next message, Jurist, this is your mother, call me when you get in I've been having some strange feelings. I love you. Call me soon."

Computerized voice, "Message saved next message, Hello Mr. Johnson I called you because Mrs. Courtland has you listed as a local contact person. Mrs. Courtland has been in an accident, and we're hoping you can come to the General Hospital as soon as possible. Ask for Dr. Stamos." Jurist immediately, hung up the phone, and rushed out the door.

Chapter 33
A Soul without a Mate

JURIST RAN INTO THE EMERGENCY ROOM. As he gasps for air he glanced around, and observes the register's desk. "Excuse me! I need to speak to Dr. Stamos concerning Shayla Courtland." The receptionist responds, "And you are."

He answered, "Jurist Johnson."

"Wait here I'm going to call him now. The receptionist picked up the phone, "Dr. Stamos please report to the emergency room waiting area."

As he waits for the doctor, Jurist paced the floor until the doctor walked in. To Jurist it feels as if the doctor is taking forever. Dr. Stamos entered the room in a sturdy pace. Jurist walked over to him, "Dr. Stamos, I'm Jurist Johnson; you called me regarding Shayla Courtland. Is she okay? What happened?"

"She was in a car accident, and I'm going to be honest with you things don't look good. She has massive trauma to the head, and neck area, we were able to stop the bleeding from the cut on her left side, and we are now waiting for the x-rays to return to see if there is any internal bleeding. As soon as we can pin point were the hemorrhaging is occurring in her head we are going to take her back into surgery to relieve the pressure. Right now she's unconscious but if you want to you can come back with me to see her. Do you know how to contact her family? If you can relay information to them for us that will help, I have to go back now follow me, and a nurse at the nursing station will assist you."

They walk through the white hall with its bright, white lights pass stretchers with white sheets to a room with Shayla surrounded by bright lights, and white curtains. As soon as Jurist saw her, he grabbed her hand, and a tear from his eye rolled down his cheek, and falls on her cheek as he leaned over to give her a kiss.

"Shayla, Shayla baby wake up," he said to her gently. "I know you're mad at me but baby don't get back at me like this. We have years of arguing left. Don't leave me baby, I need you. Tears are flooding down his face. "You're the only person God made for me. Come on Shayla fight it baby. Come back to me please. You know that I'm lost without you. We have so much unfinished business. What about our wedding, and the village of children, you wanted to have? I can't do this without you. You make me better. I can't know love without you," Jurist sobs.

Jurist looked at Shayla, and noticed that her eye twitched, and as soon as he began to have hope in his heart. She started to have convulsions. Jurist screamed, "No! No Shayla, no!"

The heart monitor started moving at a chaotic pace. A nurse rushed in the room. Just as she entered Shayla stopped convulsing, and a steady peee, sound is heard throughout the room and down the hall. "Excuse me sir," the nurse rushed over. "We've got flat line," she yells as she began to try to resuscitate Shayla. In total shock and awe, Jurist stood by the window in tears as the doctor, and another nurse ran into the room with a defibrillator. "Clear!" Jurist quivers as he heard the jolt, and saw what it does to Shayla's lifeless body. An electrical charging sound is heard followed by "Clear." The doctor tried again but with no different result. Everything appeared to be going in slow motion to Jurist as he helplessly watched the doctor and nurses fight to save Shayla's life. But although they fought valiantly, it wasn't long before everyone realized that God had called her spirit home. For a while, Jurist sat in the chair in the corner of the room with his face covered by his hands as he wept over the lost of his best friend and first love. Moments later the doctor came in to log an official time of death. One of the older nurses on the hall walked over to Jurist holds him, and allows him to rest his head on her shoulder. "Don't worry baby, God will see you through."

Chapter 34
Covenant of Love

WANTING TO BE ALONE, Jurist leaves the hospital before anyone arrives and heads to the place he feels most comfortable, the office. The pain of losing Shayla hunts his every thought. Like a ghost in a haunted house, memories of her continuously leap out at him over and over again.   Storming his mind and pushing his heart to critical over mass with emotions. The passion he once held so dear is drawing closer to his breakdown. Crying, sobbing, walking with his head down, and torn from anguish; Jurist balls up on the office floor, and cries himself to sleep. The next morning after a massive search for him, Isis finds him passed out on the floor. "Jurist, Jurist wake up everyone is looking for you," she said as she gently shakes him.

A slight sense of hope that the entire ordeal was a dream stilly passes through Jurist. "Huh." But five little words from Isis lips quickly trigger the misery of the night.

"Jurist, I am so sorry." Anger erupted from Jurist inner most life force.

"Sorry, Sorry," Jurist repeats angrily. "My future wife, mother of my children, my world is gone and all you can say is sorry. Leave me alone. Tell everyone I said to just leave me alone."
As serene as someone would approach an untamed lion, Isis moves closer towards him, "Jurist, I know this has to be hard for you, but no way am I going to leave you alone at a time like this."

"Didn't you hear me? I just want to be alone." In the back of his mind, Jurist momentarily places some of the blame of Shayla's death on Isis. He thought back to the times that Shayla revealed her distrust of Isis and her intentions. But before he reacted he simply asked her to give him time to grieve by himself. "Well I can't do that just yet. Have you talked to your mother I'm sure she wants to talk to you?" You are not the only person grieving you know, we all loved Shayla, and we are all worried about you."

"Trust me, I'm ok I just need some time alone, please."

"Well, I'll go, and let everyone know you're ok, but I'll be back in a little bit with some food."

As Isis leaves Jurist noticed the envelope with the letter he intended for Shayla to have inside it. At the top of the letter was the words "A Covenant of Love." His throat became dry, and his eyes began to water as he started reading it to himself:

To my ebony doll, wife of my soul, and comrade of my heart; I feel as though I'm traveling down a river of tears with banks of sadness surrounding my fears. It's like I'm lost in the darkness of what use to be my heart. Searching for utopia, but knowing not where to start. My spirit has eclipsed that of my soul, and I'm desperately seeking you to hold. Every minute I'm compelled to visualize how beautiful you are. I can't stop thinking of your Florida sun colored skin, rosy pink lips, and hair like silk. My mind is hung, sprung waiting for the next time I can hear you speak from your well-mannered tongue. You quenched my thirst for affection, and I will gladly trade my soul for your protection. Life is what I am missing. Like the rain that falls upon forgotten volcanoes to fill cracks, becoming veins causing such a wonderful change in its perception that is what you did to me. I must have flipped out, and gone madly insane to think that I could give you the pleasures you needed to maintain? Was it the way you glided through these hallways of life, elegantly swift, it isn't a myth, you are my queen in a story that has yet to be written. I am slipping, presenting myself with a challenge that is dangerously close, unattainable for most, and you are a celestial ghost that haunts me in my dreams. I feel like a fiend getting high off the imaginary steam we create together. Passion is what I am missing. Bring that which helps you grace my path closer to my face so I can taste satisfaction. An erotic almost psychotic perfection is my selection for tonight's resurrection of love. That is what I'm missing. I'm only wishing for your permission to work for you, and accomplish a mission that has continued for far too long. And although I'll continue to stay strong you are what I am missing...

Forever the Mate to your Soul;

Jurist

Chapter 35
Ever-After Pain

MR. SHARRIEFF TRIED HIS BEST TO CONSOLE JURIST but nothing he said or did helped to ease the burning pain in Jurist's heart. As a matter of fact, it did just the opposite because for each kind word Mr. Sharrieff spoke to him, Jurist felt more, and more guilt. Jurist had rather Mr. Sharrieff condemn, and blame him, than shower him with as he saw it, unworthy pity and pacification. After the funeral, Jurist became somewhat of a hermit evading visitors, and phone calls for days at a time. Even Nandi his mother barely heard from him. So she continuously prayed to God to help Jurist see through the pain. Having dealt with the lost of a husband, Shayla's death struck her deeply as well. Nandi revered Shayla as both a daughter and den mother of Jurist. Nandi herself imagined them creating a new generation.   But the Johnson family was not the only ones directly affected by this tragic accident. Even BAM moved at a sluggish pace at best. The projects that Shayla and Jurist were working on became almost none existent. This presented some new issues of concern for the Council of the New Future Association. They had invested a lot into the grooming process of Jurist, and ensuring his rise to the top of the organization. There was great concern as to the mental perseverance of Jurist, and his ability to rise above the agony of losing a loved one. So Professor Conan was charged with the responsibility to provide a final evaluation regarding Jurist capacity to return to leadership. In the eyes of the Council, a leader of such a monumental movement must be able to keep his wits about him in face of adversities such as these and draw strength from them. This was truly a test of Jurist's resoluteness and sense of purpose. Professor Conan, a staunch believer in Jurist, knew he had to do something immediately, and get Jurist out of this state of grief fast.

That being the case, Professor Conan picked Jurist up one afternoon, and brought him to his home.

"Would you like something to drink," he asked Jurist as he made himself a stiff drink. "No thanks, I'm not thirsty."

"Jurist, I know this past month has been hard for you, it hurts to lose someone close to you. But Jurist you have to get back on track with your life. You didn't die in that accident, as much as you wish you would have, you didn't. A person's character can be tested in many ways, and granted you have had many test in your life, but that's no reason for you to quit now. Life itself is nothing but a series of attempts to accomplish meaningful goals. How many of your goals have you successfully completed? Although what happened to your father and Shayla may seem like tragic events, you have the opportunity to make their lives more meaningful. You still have the capacity to fulfill a prophecy that both of them wanted to be accomplished by any means necessary; even if it meant them sacrificing their lives."

With tears slowly beginning to trickle down his face Jurist responds with a cracked voice, "But Omar it hurts, it hurts so much, and I don't know what I want to do. No matter how I try I can't get rid of this feeling of guilt. I can't even sleep without having nightmares. That night just keeps replaying in my head over and over again."

Professor Conan quickly wipes a tear from his eye lash. "Jurist, I've never showed you what I'm about to show you because I was never sure how you would handle it. But I want you to take a good look at this picture." Professor Conan walked over to his desk and pulled out a hand size photo of Nandi, Pharaoh, and himself and passes it to Jurist.

"Professor, that's you with my mom and dad. Why you never mentioned that you knew them personally?" Then Jurist pondered to himself why didn't my mother mention anything.

"Prior to now I didn't think it was time to reveal this information."

"Well, why show them to me now?"

"I wanted to explain to you the type of man and dear friend your father was, and the type of man you are. Pharaoh was a very fearless man, and determined to see rapid change. At times, I didn't know who he was mad at most, our oppressors or the people that didn't fight against them. He carried a lot of anger within him, that is, until he met your mother. She brought out the best in him. I wouldn't be the man I am today if it wasn't for the both of them. I can sincerely say that Pharaoh was the best friend I ever had. You see your father, and yourself are not very different. Except for the fact that you are far greater prepared to win the war that he, and many others during his time could only dream of winning. Jurist you have to understand, there have been thousands of revolutionaries that lived the lives that chose them, and every last one of them had to face seemingly insurmountable odds or horrific defeats for you to have the opportunities you have today. Disregard the time that has come to past. You and your generation are the measuring rods of their success. Remember that when you walk in a restaurant and receive service, when you walk into the men's restroom, when you go to vote, when you consider yourself more than a piece of property, think about that and the many lives that perished by whips, nooses and bullets, before you decide to walk away from our fight."

"So, you and my father were that close ha."

"We were closer than you could ever imagine."

Suddenly, as if Jurist had been given a shot of adrenaline, he rose up, "I got to go."

"Go where? I thought."

Jurist interrupts Professor Conan's sentence, "I don't know yet. But I'll know when I get there. Do you mind if I borrow your car?"

"No, but are you sure you are okay? Did I say something to upset you?"

"No, no Professor I just need to go, and clear some things up, that's all."

Professor Conan hands Jurist the keys, looked him in his eyes, and said with great conviction, "Peace be within you."

Chapter 36
Revelation

JURIST RIDES AROUND FOR A MOMENT trying to wrap his mind around the new found information that Professor Conan had provided him. Suddenly, Jurist decides to fly home. So he drives to the airport, and catches the first flight to West Palm Beach. Within hours, Jurist is in West Palm Beach, and pulling up at his mother's house in a rental car. Nandi, recently getting home herself had just begun her routine preparations to unwind after work when she hears someone at her front door.

"Who is it," she called out.

"It's me."

"Me. Who is Me?" She said as she opened her door.

"Then as if Jesus Christ had appeared himself she looked upon her son's face, and thought 'Amen, Thank God.' "Jurist, Baby! Where have you been? What you doing here?"

Jurist hugs Nandi, and pulled her in the house, "Ma, we need to talk."

They walked to the kitchen, and Jurist pulled out a chair for his mother to sit in. "Have a seat Ma, I have something to show."

Jurist shows Nandi the picture of her, Professor Conan, and his father. "Ma, why didn't you tell me Pharaoh and Professor Conan were friends?"

"So you know."

"Know what? No ma, I don't know how about you tell me."

"Baby you have to understand, the times were very different back then. Everything had to look right, and stay correct in the eyes of the public; otherwise nobody would listen to the message. If you were a community leader you weren't allowed to make mistakes."

Jurist now realizing that there is more to this story than he had previously thought became a little confused, and anxious for more information.

"Ma, I'm not following you. What you trying to tell me?"

"Jurist, David or Professor Omar Conan as you know him, wasn't just your father's friend he was my friend as well. I knew this day would eventually come to pass." Nervously, she began rubbing her hands together. "Jurist, Omar, Omar is your biological father."

In total shock Jurist stood up and hollered, "What! Hell nall. Ma what, I mean, what you mean Omar is my biological father," he said in a condescending voice. "No ma, you are not telling me this right now."

"Baby, I was young, David was intelligent, and wealthy, and ready to bring change to our community. But he was already married, and if it had got out that he was the father of my child that would have killed the spirit of the movement. Pharaoh and I became reacquainted before I found out that I was pregnant, and after he

175

found out he said that he didn't care. He told me that he loved me, and that he would raise you as his own. We decided that it would be best for all of us if we kept it between us. So, David left, and Pharaoh stayed here with me to raise you."

"So, ya'll think it was better to lie not just to me but to an entire community. Ma, how could you do something like that? How could you choose to make my life an eternal lie, and say it was for the best; the best for who Ma?" Nandi hides her face in her hands as she cries. "Look at me, look at me, do it still look like it was the best thing to do. Ha, Ma? My entire life I've grown up thinking that my father was dead and that was what was best for me. I can't believe this. And who came up with this brilliant idea to ruin my life, David, if that's his real name. I bet he didn't want to lose his righteous image with bad publicity.

"No, sweetheart don't blame David, it was me. I made him promise never to say anything to anyone especially you. I was scared Jurist."

Jurist looked down over his mother as she sat and cried, "Ma, you weren't scared, you were just ashamed."

"Baby, you have to believe me, at the time it did seem like the right thing to do."

"Are you sure Ma, are you sure that you did all this for me? I got to get out of here."

Nandi continued to cry and scream don't go as Jurist stormed out of the house.

Chapter 37
Swing Rules

CONFUSED AND DISTRAUGHT JURIST DRIVES through one of the more violent areas of his hometown community. After a while he stopped at one of the most decrepit looking parks one can envision. As he stopped on the side of the street, he surveys the area, and scrutinizes the deplorable conditions. Dirt, broken bottles and trash cover the sporadic patches of grass. A flimsy rusted out fence surrounds the park. A broken refrigerator, large pile of garbage, and a mattress that reeks of piss is perched at the corner of the so-called park. The smell of the mattress is so repugnant stray dogs don't even attempt to eat the recently trashed food thrown away by the residents near the park. Neighbor after neighbor, walk across the street to the nauseating mound to discard their waste. Yet still Jurist braves the trek into this playground of rubbish. He looked over the swing set that used to have three swings, and he walked to it as he reminisces about his mother, and how she used to push him in the very same swing set. He sat in between the cold rusted chains, and onto the crack rubber seat. Then he looked up at the sky, and poses a question to God. But as he questions God a young boy walked up to the swing set, and stood by Jurist as Jurist sat in the only available swing. Jurist didn't even notice the boy as he walked up. "God, I don't know what to do. I can't take all this. Why me Lord, why I got to go through all this?"

"You finished," the boy asked Jurist?

A little bit uneasy by the way the little boy was able to walk up to him completely unnoticed, "What you said Li Man?"

Boldly the boy said, "It's my turn, you stopped, so that means it's my turn, that's the rules. Whenever you stop somebody else gets to go. It's my turn since you stopped."

"Okay, my bad, here you go." Jurist hands over the swing to Li Man.

"I bet I can swing higher than you can." At a young age the streets had already taught Li Man to hustle any and everybody when the opportunity presents itself. Because although Jurist had not noticed Li Man, Li Man had taken notice to Jurist before he got out of his car.

"Oh, yeah."

"Yeah, I saw how high you could go when I was waiting. And to be so big you can't go too high. What you scared of? I used to be scared to go too high. I thought that I might flip out and fall. Then my brother told me that I just had to hold on tight and not be afraid. Watch, I'll show you."

The little boy started swinging as hard as he could. With strong dips and leans, Li Man began swinging higher and higher.

"You can swing pretty high."

"I told you. Watch this."

Li Man swings up as high as he could, and as he reached his highest point he jumped from the swing, and landed on his feet, nearly landing on a broken bottle.

"See you can go real high, and if you're not afraid to jump you don't have to worry about falling. If I could, I would do a complete three sixty."

From across the street a woman is heard screaming, "Jay, Jay get your behind over here right now."

"I got to go, my Mama don't like me playing over here she said it's too dangerous."

"You should listen to your Mama. "Hey Li Man here." Jurist gave Jay Jay a dollar as he began to run home.

"Thanks for lesson Li Man."

Li Man looked back at him and said, "Thanks, you should practice, and try to see how high you can go."

"All right, I just might do that. Li Man began to run off again when Jurist called him back, "Hey Li Man. Here," Jurist hands him another dollar, "Give this to your brother."

With a sad look in his eye Li Man said "I can't."

"Why not?"

"He died last year. He got shot right there."

Li Man points at the spot to the left of Jurist where there is a missing swing. Then Jay Jay's mother called for him again.

"Here I come, Ma."

"Be safe Li Man," Jurist whispered.

After Li Man leaves, Jurist sat back in the swing, and started to swing, and as soon as he got as high as he could he looked to the sky and screamed, "I heard you," as he jumped out of the swing. Jurist drives back home and reconciles with his mother.

Chapter 38
Fallen Thoughts

WHILE ON THE PLANE BACK TO TALLAHASSEE, Jurist
pondered scores of questions that he wanted answers to; even
though the trip home helped to make some things clearer for him
the anger, hurt, and betrayal Jurist had for his newfound father had
yet to subside. And by the time Jurist had reached Professor
Conan's home that resentment had reached its boiling point.
Unaware of the rage that was just beyond his front door, Professor
Conan attempted to retreat to his study to review some journals.
Then suddenly he hears, "BOOM Boom Boom." The Professor is
alarmed by the loud knocking at the door. "BOOM BOOM Boom."
"Who is it?" he screamed. "BOOM, BOOM BOOM." Totally rattled
by the beating he became very anxious when he realizes who had
been drumming at his door. Without formally speaking, Jurist
walked by the Professor slightly shoving him to the side with his
forearm. The first words out of Jurist mouth, "We need to talk."
Jurist continues to walk back into Professor Conan's study, and
began to pace around the room.

"This room is where you look at the present, and envision the future

right," he cynically said to the Professor. "Well then, tell me what you planned for today."
Inquisitively, Professor Conan asked, "What you talking about Jurist?"

"Don't bullshit me Omar or should I say David. You know exactly what I'm talking about. Why didn't you tell me? You give me all this talk about loyalty and trust but you never once thought to tell me that I was your son. How can you even consider yourself a man when you knowingly left a widow to take care of your son by herself with no support?"

"Hold on Jurist, let me explain." Professor Conan still in awe of the way Jurist bombarded him with questions, tried to calm Jurist down. "Honestly Jurist, I have sat in this room thousands of times and thought about what I would say to you at this very moment, but I never came up with an answer better than the truth."

"Yeah right you hypocrite, now you suddenly know how to tell the truth."

"Jurist the number one challenge of a leader of any kind is hypocrisy."

"I don't know if you realize this or not but I don't want to hear any more of your bogus lectures."

"Son, just listen to me,"

"Son! Don't you dare call me son! You don't know me like that."

"Jurist, at the time we couldn't risk people not understanding that your mother and Pharaoh had fallen deeply in love in spite of the fact that she carried my child. You don't think it was hard for me to leave knowing that you were my son. I traded the love of my child for the love of my people. Does that make me a hypocrite? The situation in itself seemed almost ordained."

"You trying to tell me that in some way you feel that God intended for me to grow up fatherless? How twisted are you?"
"Jurist, remember when I told you that your father was an angry man."

In a condescending tone Jurist replies, "Yeah so what, everybody was mad back then. Blacks had it bad?"

"Yes, but some had it worst than others and Pharaoh was one of them. When Pharaoh and I were young men about the same age you are now. We decided to ride to Atlanta to attend a march. But before we could make it, I stopped in this little hick town to get some gas. The Whites only sign had been knocked down so we couldn't see it. I got out and began pumping the gas, while Pharaoh went inside to pay for it and to get us something to drink. After I finished pumping the gas I got back in the car. As I sat in the car I started to become impatient, and wondered what he was doing."
Professor Conan started to have a flashback.

"Damn Pharaoh, what's taking you so long? I got out the car, and walked in the store. But when I went inside I saw nobody not even Pharaoh. So I went back to the car to get the shotgun that my father gave me before we left. I walked around the back, and bared witness to an ungodly ritual. I saw Pharaoh laying on his back unconscious with his mouth gagged, and three white men standing over him with a knife. One of the men stood up and said 'Now nigger I have your manhood,' as he raised Pharaoh's penis and testicles over his head. I started shooting in the air, and they ran into the woods. After all these years I still wish I'd killed every last one of them. I picked Pharaoh up, and carried him to the car, and drove as fast as I could to the nearest hospital. Needless to say he lived but he never fully recovered. Your mother was the only woman Pharaoh ever told about that night. I thought that for Pharaoh to fall in love with the same woman I had committed adultery, and secretly conceived a child with was fate. I knew he would love you as his own therefore I didn't put up much resistance when your mother asked me not to tell anyone that you were my child. It was like God had given me the opportunity to right a wrong. I never truly forgave myself for what happened to Pharaoh so I gave my best friend my first born son."

"But after Pharaoh got killed why didn't you come back to claim me as your own."

"I tell myself I didn't because I felt that I owed it to your mother to let her decide whether or not she wanted to tell you, but looking at you right now I know that I was just too scared to tell you myself. But over these last couple of years I've gotten to know the young man you've up grown to be, and I see that your mother did a wonderful job, and I wish with all my heart that I could have played a larger role in it but everything happens for a reason."

"So what do we do now? Where do we go from here?"

"We have to live with this gift called the present, and I'm going to do everything in my power to help you lead the people that are waiting to follow you."

"That's the thing, I don't know if I can lead these people I don't even know where I'm going." Jurist walked over to the chair and sat down.

"I know it's a scary position, to be expected to have the correct answer to every question while knowing your own shortcomings and failures. But a wise man once said that "Every major decision can look like a failure without hindsight but the risk you take to make it succeed is success in itself. So don't get caught up in every decision being right or wrong because sometimes it's the choices we don't make that defines us better than the choices we do make. Omar paused for a second, and stopped walking around. He sat in the chair next to Jurist looked him in the eyes and said, "I said all that to say this, just hold true to the beat of your soul, and your inner most thoughts, and not only will I follow you but the people, the people will gladly risk their lives to support the vision that God himself has given you."

Jurist stood up from of his seat and walked away, "I don't know Omar I need some time to think things clear, at least for myself." Jurist began to walk out, and Omar gave chase, and stopped him before he exited the room, "Well maybe this story about your grandfather and I will help you see things a little clearer."

Chapter 39
To Lead or Not To Lead

"I WAS BORN THE SON OF A PREACHER and by being born
the son of a preacher man I feel I was blessed with the gift of sight.
When I say sight, I don't mean that I had some sort of super power
that enables me to be prophetic in any way. I mean it in a visionary
manner, so to speak. Through the divined sanction and approval of
our Lord God, and the unyielding faith of my father, and his
churchly flock, I was granted sight through the hundreds of pairs of
eyes that religiously listened to my father's words as he interpreted
the words of their God to them, not only on the day of the Sun but
the six days prior as well. Because of his superior relationship with
their God, people invested much of their time and service to his
ministry. In return, they would offer or ask that he take secured
glimpses into their lives. Although a strong man six foot two
inches, two hundred and five pounds of intelligence, charisma,
dedication and honesty, I could never get over the fact that he was
all those things, and even more important to me, he was my father.
And let me tell you, being the son of a preacher man is no easy job.
For starters, I had to help set up for any and every event that was
sponsored or co-sponsored by my father's church. But that was by
far my easiest task because being the son of the preacher man also

meant that I would need to get ready to preside as he did over the hundreds of people that depended upon him and his message from their God. But I had not yet heard God speak to me. On numerous occasions I heard my father speak of his conversations with God. So I asked my father one-day, I said, 'Daddy, I have watched you preach for years and years, and I have patiently studied his words as you preferred, but I still haven't heard the voice of your God.' Then my father told me something that has stuck with me ever since. He said, 'David, you will never hear my God.' I couldn't believe what I was hearing. How could a man that had basically devoted our lives to teaching others the words of his and their God tell his one and only son that he would never hear his God?

As much as his answer confused me, it intrigued me all the same. Therefore, I asked him, 'Don't you consider yourself to be a noble man?'

He responded in his never changing solemn voice, 'Nobility is an everyday challenge that is measurable by the accomplishments of one's life, but upon my death, I do hope that I will have lived a life recognized by the people who knew me best to be worthy of nobility.' You see, that was the thing about my father."

Professor Conan walked around Jurist who was sitting at the time, and put his hands on both Jurist's shoulders, "Your grandfather. I could never get a straight answer from him. Leaving me with the ambiguous job of figuring out what he meant.

Relentless in my quest to find out why he felt that his God would not speak to me as he had spoken to him, I then asked him, 'Isn't it the job of a son to follow the footsteps of his father?'

He nodded his head, and responded, 'Yes, if following the father's footsteps is what the son wishes to follow, and if the father's footsteps are righteous, and deserves to be followed.'

After making several more vague attempts to get my father to answer my question, and tell me why his God, and the God of his people would not speak to me I became resolute in my questioning.

'Daddy, I'm for real. If your God don't speak to me, how will I learn to lead my people?' To this day I remember the stunned, searching look on my father's face. Then he answered, 'Son, the people I lead today, and the people you will lead tomorrow are not, and will not be the same. It is not my God or the Gods of others that you must listen for, for you have your own God within you that you must listen to.'

Confused by his answer I immediately answered back, 'But the Bible said that there is but one God.'

'I know what the Bible said, but the truth as I know it to be about the Bible, and any other religious book for that matter, is that they are books, stories, a journal so to speak. It reflects the thoughts of the past, and teaches us vital lessons about the integrity of good people, and the deceitfulness, and treachery of evil people that live amongst us. Different religions represent the different lifestyles or customs of that particular group of people. Take me for example, as a preacher, I provide a place of worship for the good, and the opportunity for people to be redeemed for their evil or wrong doings. But it's not my job as a preacher that determines my connection with God it's my job as a person.'

"That day, I walked away from my father even more confused than before, so I went to the source of my confusion, the Bible, and I found my way."

Then Jurist intercedes, "So, Professor what is your way? What goals do you have for yourself and the people that follow you?" "To help! To help the evil and wicked people of this nation gain their redemption. Take your time son the liberation isn't going anywhere, and neither am I."

Days later, Jurist is resting and reminiscing about the talk he had with Professor Conan. Trying to put everything in order was a difficult puzzle for Jurist to say the least. All of a sudden Jurist got the urge to walk. Jurist walked from one part of town to the next. His only stop was to a convenience store to get a bottle of water to drink. He took mental pictures of homes, businesses, schools, and churches that he passed along the way. He gazed at the children as some of them made their way into their homes as it grew dark. Then when he passed a group of teenagers congregating at another convenience store about a mile away from the store he brought his water from. The manager of the store got into an argument with one of the boys who tried to buy a cigar. The manager refused to sell the young man a cigar so he became upset, and started cursing out the manager. Jurist put his head down, and continued to walk.

Jurist then passed a bus spot where prostitutes usually hang out, and pick up tricks. There were two people working the bus stop this evening. One was a woman who looked to be sprung out on drugs. The other was a gay man with a tight yellow skirt on. As Jurist began to cross the street towards the prostitute Jurist spots a little boy riding his tricycle less than thirty feet away from the bus stop. But Jurist saw no parents or other children with the child. So Jurist walked over to the child, and asked him where his parents were, and where he lived. The little boy couldn't have been over three years old. The gay man saw Jurist talking to the boy, and noticed that Jurist had some concern for the child. So he yelled out to Jurist, and told him that the little boy stayed in the house about five houses down the road. Jurist decided to walk the little boy home.

Thinking that someone would be concerned that the child had wondered off so far, and it had gotten dark pretty quickly. The house had a broken down fence around it. Jurist watched the child until he got to the front door. Jurist then screamed out as he saw someone through the screen door of the home. "Hey, your little boy is at the door." A teenage girl walked out the door.

"What you said," she asked Jurist.

Jurist responded, "I was just letting you know that your son was outside. He was all the way down the road by the bus stop."

The girl responded, "Oh yeah, he ride down there all the time. The people down there know him. They know he stay here. They watch out for him. I tell him not to leave the yard but that boy don't listen to nobody."

Sadness gripped Jurist heart as he walk away from the house. As Jurist walked away he found himself traveling down a road with no lights. There were woods on both sides of the road, and on one side there was a canal. It was too dark to see much of anything else. All types of thoughts ran around Jurist head as he thought about the reaction the girl had, and the neglectful life in which that child had to grow up in. At the end of the shadowy road there was a church. The church was abandoned, and had a couple of windows knocked out of it. Yet still, Jurist felt compelled to walk up to the porch of the church. Jurist fell to his knees, and began to pray. He prayed for the community, that child, and the children who were suffering similar fates. He asked God for the strength to change the things he could change, and the power to make a permanent change for righteousness. Jurist asked God to guide him, and clean his soul. Most important Jurist asked God to save his soul, and the soul of the people that lived in these hopeless communities. As Jurist raised his head, and washed away the tears he wept a single tear fell to that hallowed ground. Soon after, a hunched over street light flickered, and eventually lit up. Jurist turned around, took a couple steps towards the light, and stared at it for a moment. When he turned back around to walk away he noticed that the name of the church was Redemptive Life of Friendship Church of God. With a renewed spirit Jurist began his walk home.

When Jurist made it home he checked his answering machine, and noticed that he had a message. The message was from Professor Conan. He told Jurist that he had something very important to tell him, and that he was going to come, and pick him up at Ten O'clock tonight. Jurist looked at his clock, and saw that it was already a half passed nine. He immediately rushed into the shower, and prepared for Professor Conan. As he suspected exactly at Ten O'clock Professor Conan was knocking at his door. Going commando Jurist threw on a pair of jeans, a t-shirt, and opened the door, "Would you like to come in." The Professor answered back, "Not really, however I would like it if you put on some shoes, and meet me at my car."

"Okay, just give me a second."

When Jurist got to the car he noticed that Mr. Sharrieff was on the passenger side of the car.

Surprised to see Mr. Sharrieff he paid little attention to the other gentlemen in the backseat. "Get in and close the door," the Professor urged Jurist.

"Mr. Sharrieff, it's good to see you."

"It's good to see you as well Jurist."

The Professor intercepts their conversation. "Jurist, the gentleman to your left has a blindfold that he is going to hand to you. I want you to take the blindfold, and put it over your eyes."

Shook by Professor Conan's request Jurist responds, "You want me to do what."

"Put the blindfold on," Mr. Sharrieff answered.

"For what, where we going?"

Mr. Sharrieff said in a demanding, yet calm voice, "Jurist you just have to trust us."

Hesitantly, Jurist places the blindfold over his eyes, and ties them. Mr. Sharrieff turned the music up, and they drive off. When they reach their destination, Mr. Sharrieff instructs Jurist to keep his blindfold on. Then all three doors open and close. A couple of minutes pass then Jurist hears Professor Conan's voice through a loud speaker tell him to exit the car. Jurist opened the door, and steps out the car. "Can I take off this blindfold now," he shouted. "Yes, you may." Jurist took off his blindfold, and at the same time

the car is driven off. Greetings Jurist, and welcome to the world of
the seeing," Professor Conan said to him. As Jurist eyes adjust to
the bright lights that are shine down upon him.

"Where am I?"

"Exactly where you're supposed to be, my son. We have brought
you here so you can claim your birthright."

"We, who are these people?"

"These men are members of the Council, and more importantly they
will be your brothers and eternal friends. As soon as you take the
oath, and accept challenge."

"I can barely see any of ya'll, those lights are blinding me."

"Trust me Jurist that's just a temporary affect, as soon as you
complete the challenges, and take the oath you will gain prefect
vision."

"But I don't know if I am ready."

Jurist recognized Mr. Sharrieff's voice as he said, "Don't be
frightened Jurist, for this moment trust your heart, and do the best
you can do."

Then an unrecognizable voice asked Jurist, "Are you ready to take
the challenge."

"With conviction Jurist responds, "I am."

"Jurist is taking through several enduring challenges, and when he
gets to the last challenge he is greeted by a group of eight men
surrounding him on the north, south, east and west of him. Then
the presiding chancellor steps in front of Jurist, and said to him in a
simple voice, "What is it you want for your people, and give me the
only the answer that is in your heart."

From his knees, Jurist had flashbacks of all the mental pictures he gathered on his walk today, and he roared, "I want my people to be free."

The Chancellor then told Jurist, "Arise and shine your light on the world as bright as the light shined upon you as you first took off your blindfold."

Professor Conan, walked up to Jurist and said, "For you and me life is not promised but don't be afraid my son. Just give your whole heart, and do the best you can, and you will free our people, and your brothers are here to help you. Jurist looked around the warehouse, and saw hundreds of men in suits.

Mr. Sharrieff yelled, "Progress through Knowledge," and everyone in the stands hollered back, "Prosperity through Freedom."

Chapter 40
Workaholic

AS THE YEARS PASSED, Jurist worked avidly for the Black
Action Movement, and NFA while continuing to excel in every other
facets of his life except for love. Randomly, he would talk to his
mother, and if it had not been for Ermine his trips home would
have become even scarcer. Like an ant, Jurist worked, and worked
burying himself in his task as a means of dealing with the pain of
losing Shayla. In spite of all that transpired, Jurist and Professor
Conan began to forge a bond. Not the typical father son bond but a
bond nonetheless. Jurist was making Professor Conan very proud
by dedicating his life to the goals of the Council. All the Council was
concerned with was the passion and wherewithal Jurist possessed
as he led this new movement. Year after year Jurist support within
the community grew, and so did membership. Jurist organized
rallies across the entire State of Florida.

Jurist created avenues for voices of forgotten streets and
neighborhoods. He marched in the darkness of night up and down
criminalized street shedding light on the perversely traditional ways
people were forced to make a living. In exchange for volunteer
services he found legitimate jobs for ex-convicts. He supplied safe

housing to women of abuse and new clothes for unfortunate children. He provided breaths of life to drown-out and unconscious communities. Before long, a membership of tens became hundreds, and an organization of one became a dozen. The Council watched over Jurist as a curator would a revered museum, gathering mostly anonymous gifts, grants and awards which allowed him to expand, and make good on public promises. This type of endorsement made Jurist all the more ambitious. Every now and then he and Mr. Sharrieff would meet to discuss life, and the responsibilities of leadership. For some reason talking with Mr. Sharrieff made Jurist feel clairvoyant at times. He felt closer to Shayla, and more at peace with himself. Mr. Sharrieff's presence reminded him of the pure intentions he and Shayla had for one another.

A year or so after Shayla's passing, Isis and Jurist started working closely with one another and Jurist had some guilt resonating within him over it. However, Mr. Sharrieff advised Jurist that he had no fault in what happened and that he needed forgiveness from no one, and he employed Jurist to forgive himself. But whenever Mr. Sharrieff would talk about Jurist forgiving himself Jurist would escape by saying he has to get back to his work. And for the next three years no one worked harder for down trodden communities, and people without hope than Jurist. But Jurist's success in Florida did not impede him from attempting to flourish elsewhere. Jurist felt that his best opportunity to make change was in Washington, DC the nation's capital. Jurist had faith that all the effort, and success he had in Tallahassee, and throughout Florida was just a microcosm for what was in store when he reached Washington. As a matter of fact, one of the only losses he suffered while in Florida was the rejection for a plan to implement the Reclamation for Minority, and Economically Challenged Prisoners program nationwide.

Jurist saw this rejection as a direct challenge to the effectiveness of his program. For years Jurist worked hand and hand with volunteers and local businesses to rehabilitate and change the devastating effect of imprisonment of young black youth. For that reason, with the approval of the Council Jurist moved to D.C, opened a small law firm, and immediately started a local Black Action Movement Chapter with the Reclamation for Minority, and Economically Challenged Prisoners program listed as its primary program. Many things had changed but one thing has remained the same, Isis continued to be a faithful friend, and diligent partner of Jurist. Many people suspected that they shared something more than friendship they both continued to deny any such involvement. The truth of the matter is that the Council would prefer them to become more affectionate with one another to service as an exemplary couple to the rest of the organization, and solidify a union of hierarchy. However, Jurist's main concern was gaining national support for the Reclamation for Minority, and Economically Challenged Prisoners program, and getting Ermine out of prison. Jurist and Isis are currently at their office and Isis is gathering papers, and placing them in the file room. As soon as she finishes collating the files, her phone rang.

"Yes, this is Isis speaking."

"Isis, do you have the Brown files in your office?"

"Yes I do Jurist. Do you need them?"

"No, I was just making sure I didn't misplace them."

"You couldn't misplace those files if you wanted to. What time do you have?"

"A half past noon."

"I'll bring them down to your office." Isis grabbed Ermine's files, and took them to Jurist. Playfully she said to him, "Here are your files King Jurist."

"Ha, Ha, Ha very funny," he sarcastically responds.

"What you doing?"

"Nothing, just looking over my notes for the meeting tonight."

"Have you eaten anything?"

"Not since last night."

"Come on, let's go, and grab something to eat. Let me get my purse, and I'll meet you out front."

Isis went and grabbed her purse from her office then walked to her car. Jurist opened the passenger side door and slides into the seat. "Damn Jurist! It took you long enough. The line is going to be long as hell by time we get there messing around with you."

"If it were up to me I would have skipped lunch today anyway."

"No you wouldn't, today is jerk chicken, greens and macaroni day."

"Well, what's taking you so long," he said to her with a grin on his face?

When they arrive at the restaurant they are quickly greeted. "Welcome to *Jasper's*. Mr. Johnson we are a little packed right now but I will get you and Mrs. Nahash a seat as soon as I can." As they wait they began to talk about the business they have at hand.

Jurist asked her, "Is everything ready for Wednesday's meeting with the Prison Board?"

"Yes. Everything is in order."

"Were you able to get the reporters we wanted to do the interview?"

"Yes, but we probably won't get no more than two minutes tops."

"That's not enough to get the word out."

The waitress approaches them, "Mr. Johnson, Ms. Nahash your

table is ready." As they walk to the table they continue to talk.

"Don't worry Jurist, after we get the Prison Board to back BAM the Reclamation for Minority, and Economically Challenged Prisoners program will be able to make a serious impact nationwide. Giving us the recognition we need."

"I'm not worried about the Prison Board. We will let the statistics speak for themselves. If four additional years of service, and two-thousand prison members with only a 2.5% recidivism rate don't grab their attention nothing will."

Chapter 41
Can Butterflies Swim

WITHIN THE CAR, it was a silent ride that seems to take forever. Jurist drove as if he was programmed R&B drone. Leaning to the side with one hand on the steering wheel, and the other with his chin nestled on the interior portion of his left thumb he looked cooler than a pimp riding down the street in his brand new Cadillac. Since leaving the office he and Isis had probably only spoken ten sentences to one another. Quite the opposite, outside the car it was total chaos. The roads were packed; people were walking in and out of traffic acting as if they owned the road. Yet still, Jurist remained calm. Isis on the other hand had to rub her hands together to keep them from shaking. While she tried her best, pretending to search for papers to disguise how sick she was feeling, she could not control the butterflies that had infiltrated her stomach. To take her mind off the tremendous job that was ahead of both of them, she decided to try to peruse some reports and statistics. Every now and then she would raise her head and take a deep breath. At a stop light about two miles from their destination she took a glance at Jurist and wondered to herself.

"How can a man that has his life's work riding in the hands of people he do not know or trust be so calm?" Instinctively, as if he was listening to her thoughts Jurist sat upright and circumspectly. Finished with his daily gaze at the world he placed a Tupac CD into the stereo, and skipped to one of his favorite tracks. Soon after, he began singing, "Staring at the world through my rear view."

His head started to bob, and his shoulders started to swagger. The more Jurist sung the closer Isis paid attention to the lyrics. The more attention she paid to the lyrics the more her nerves dissipated, and before she knew it she wasn't nervous anymore. Watching Jurist become more and more animated, as he vibed to the music, made Isis amp up. So much so, she began reciting the chorus lines, and bouncing to the beat along with Jurist. To an on looker they would have looked like some high school hard heads skipping school riding downtown looking for some fun. Not two up and rising attorneys getting ready to present a case to the Federal Prison Board. By the time they made it to the parking lot, they were both invigorated with a renewed spirit, and as they grabbed their brief cases, and charts, Isis told Jurist 'thank you.'

Jurist was a little unsure as to why Isis was thanking him, so he asked her and she said to him, "Man, I got to be honest with you. On the way here I was so nervous I was about to throw up. I kept looking at you and you seemed to be just as calm as you could be. Then you put in that Tupac CD, and started singing and dancing, and I started to feel a lot better."

As they walked towards the building Jurist looked at Isis, and smiled. Then he told her, "When I was in high school, I had this teacher who talked me into joining the school's history academic games team that he coached. The first match I had was against a group of white kids that went to a private school. I was really nervous, and coach noticed it to. So he walked up to me and said, "Boy you look scared." I told him na'll I'm not scared but I do have a couple butterflies in my stomach. Then he told me something that I will never forget, he said the trick with butterflies is teaching them to swim, once you teach them to swim you won't have to worry about them flying around in your stomach. Naturally, I asked him the same question anyone else would; how am I supposed to do that? That's when he passed me this walkman that he had with him and said just listen. Isis asked, "What was he listening to?" Jurist responded with a smirk on his face, "Sam Cooke, It's Been a Long Time Coming. By time I finished listening, my butterflies were swimming."

"How did you do in the match," Isis asked?

"I won," Jurist responded with glee. "As a matter of fact, I only lost one game that year."

"Oh yeah, do you remember who you lost to?" Jurist paused for a second then he said, "Shayla," and he smiled.

They had reached the entrance of the building and Jurist held the door open for Isis. They walked over to the receptionist, and she advised them that their meeting was being held in room 314. They walked down the hall, and entered the elevator after a group of well groomed men in black suits exited it. Just before the elevator reached the third floor Jurist looked over at Isis and said, "So you ready?" Isis looked back at Jurist, and said with a grin on her face, "I'm just staring at the world through my rear view." They smiled at each other for a second, and the doors open. Jurist said, "Game Time."

There was a serene confidence that they both shared as they walked into the conference room. Although Jurist, and Isis had arrived at the meeting 30 minutes ahead of schedule they were surprised when they saw what looked to be the entire Federal Board Program Review committee already present. Jurist began to apologize for not getting there sooner when Mr. Frank Chaney, Deputy Director stopped him, and advised him that there was no error on his part. He told them that an issue of significant importance had come to their attention, and it was too late to cancel the appointment. So he asked Jurist if he wouldn't mind expediting their proposal request in order for them to take care of the issue. Jurist advised the committee that he and Isis could reschedule the request review for a later date. That's when the Deputy's assistant told them that the next possible date for review was six months away. Jurist's intuition told him that this was just a clever plow to create confusion so he hesitated for a split second. But as usual, Isis was on point, and immediately begin passing out the proposals. The battle had begun. Like a veteran educator teaching simple mathematics to middle school students Isis presence was demanding. In contrast, Jurist bombarded the Board like a head strong football coach providing reason after reason why a successful program like the Reclamation Program should be funded. As Isis entered into her closing remarks, Jurist surveyed the room for facial expression that could help him figure out who was interested in funding the program. Jurist glanced at the hard probing, pretentious look on the face of the Deputy Director and he knew that he was not on BAM's side. As a matter of fact, Jurist noticed no apathetic looked from any of the committee members. Their faces were as cold and pasty as the walls that surrounded the oak colored rectangle table they sat behind. Jurist felt that he would at least see some glimmer of hope from Katherine Tate, the Deputy Director's assistant, the one person whose skin resembled the surface color of the table. Nonetheless, when he peeked at her eyes to bridge the gap of empathy they returned no message of intent to support the program. When Jurist stepped closer to the committee to pass out the final statistics they would cover today. Jurist noticed that directly in front of Mrs. Tate, there was a scratch in the table that revealed that the table was only the color of oak on the surface.

Below the surface was an ivory colored artificial wood. Jurist saw the irony in the scratch on the table. Thus, with discontent lingering in his heart, Jurist watched as Isis tried to embed the most impressive, and compelling argument that BAM has in its arsenal, "Lastly, ladies and gentlemen of the board, the employment rate for released prisoners sponsored by BAM has increased at an 87% rate which is a direct result of the counseling, and job training implemented through the program. In addition, over 50% of these prisoners have received at least their GED upon graduating from the Reclamation Program. Clearly these statistics suggest that

BAM's Reclamation Program is a successful, and viable program that needs to be implemented nationwide. There are over 900,000 black men incarcerated as we speak, this Reclamation Program can make a great change with your help. Thank you for your time, and if you have any further questions you can either refer to your program proposal or you can ask me now."

As speculated Mrs. Tate was the first to ask a question. In her most proper voice she asked, "Who else will help fund such a program on a national level, an initiative like this will cost millions of dollars?"

Isis advises them, "If you take a look on page 50 of the proposal you will see a draft for a grant requesting government assistance. There is also an annual breakdown of the last two years that list all the cost incurred by BAM to keep the program running without government assistance. However, the grant only asked that the Federal Prison Board match whatever monetary figures, man hours, and technology that BAM contributes.

Anna Sparks, Senior Executive for the Program Review committee answered back, "You mean to tell me that BAM is willing, and able, to contribute half of the funds, and man hours needed to effectively run a program of this magnitude nationwide." The Deputy Director interjects, "who exactly is funding you again, and is your funding source contingent upon us agreeing to fund this program? From his previous position on the right of the podium, Jurist unnoticeably taps Isis and slides in front of the podium, "I can assure you all that BAM has a host of loyal private philanthropists, most of who are also listed within the program proposal. BAM is prepared to run smaller scale program across the Southeastern Region. However with your assistance we can set up a primary focus group ranging from 20 to 50 members in federal and state prison across the nation."

As Jurist spoke Isis observed James Ludlow, Department of Justice Deputy Assistant and Brian Reed, Federal Board of Investigations, Denise Adams, Chief Investigator of Prisons pass notes to one another. However, throughout the entire meeting neither one of them asked a single question. Isis found this to be very odd since they are members of the Program Review committee.

Becoming a little hasty after the note is passed to him. Deputy Chaney advises Isis and Jurist that they had another issue to take care of. Then he stood up, smiled and extended his hand. Jurist and Isis walked around the podium, and over to the table to shake the hands of the committee members. After shaking both their hands, the Deputy said, "Now, we will give serious consideration to your offer, and give your proposal to our lawyers for them to peruse, and you should have your preliminary answer within a month. Thank you for coming, and send our regards to the rest of your organization. On the surface, this seems to be a great opportunity for us all. We just have to go through all the red tape, you understand."

Jurist being the bold person he is asked for the committee's attention one more time. "Ladies and Gentlemen, I think it's my duty to remind you all that we have tried to acquire the cooperation of the Federal Prison Board on this matter once before without success. However, I hope that this meeting will end this stagnant reaction before it became a horrible streak of discrepancies. Thank you."

Then Jurist and Isis leave the conference room. Before Isis and Jurist can make it to the first floor to begin their interview with Channel 27, Deputy Director, Chaney began barking around commands. "Alright, I want you to find out as much information as you can about this Black Action Movement organization. That means how many real members they have, their leaders, their history, and exactly who are these philanthropists that are helping to fund them. Something's not right about this program, especially that Jurist."

Jumping to the side of the Deputy Director, Mrs. Katherine Tate quickly asked, "So do you want me to work on the legality of BAM?" "Of course that's what I want you to do," he retorts. Somewhat flabbergasted he asked, "Why don't I already know who this guy is?

They have already submitted one proposal somebody should have gotten word to me about this group. Somebody has some explaining to do. Who authorized this program to work with the prisoners in the first place? Where is the warden? Get him on the phone now; someone has some explaining to do. Katherine, make sure that one of those proposals get to the Attorney General."

Katherine asked, "Mr. Chaney are you really considering giving a pass to every prison in the nation to this group of self-righteous Black Panther wannabe?"

Deputy Director Chaney responds, "Just do your job as instructed." He grabbed his briefcase, and walked out of the room with Mr. Ludlow and Mr. Reed following him. But just as he turned the corner, Mrs. Tate rushed back to him and advises him that a news team is down stairs preparing to interview Mr. Johnson.

Chapter 42
Institutionalized Enemy

IT DOESN'T TAKE LONG FOR MR. CHANEY TO HEAD TO HIS OFFICE, and contact Samuel Gaviston, Federal Board of Investigation, Assistant Director. With his FBI henchman Brian Reed by his side, he made the call, and places it on speaker phone. You can hear his strong Kentucky accent as soon as he speaks, "Samuel, this Frank Chaney."

"Well how you doing old friend, haven't heard from you in a minute."

"Yeah, things have been pretty quiet on this part of town. However, Brian and I have a small predicament we were hoping we could get your assistance with."

 "You know me; whatever I can do for an old friend I will."

"Well are you near a TV?"

"Yeah, I got one here in my office?"

"Turn to Channel 27"

"All right."

"You see the people that Susan is about to interview. I need little more information than the report is going to give me about that organization and its leadership."

In the background as they talk Channel 27 the news reporter is conducting her interview with Jurist. "Hi, I'm Susan Luckman, and I'm speaking with Jurist Johnson, President of the organization B.A.M Black Action Movement. Mr. Johnson met with the Federal Prison Board today, and proposed a nationwide usage of their Prisoner Reclamation Program. The program was first implemented 6 years ago in Palm Beach County, FL to help young black males deal with prison life, but eventually prisoners of all races started to join. Now the program have helped over 2,000 prisoners either gain a GED or job with less than 3% of the prisoners returning back to a life of crime. Mr. Johnson, why do so many prisoners within your program seem to have so much success? Especially, since they are often reinserted back into practically the same situation, if not worst."

"Susan, The Minority and Economically Challenged Reclamation program is able to help because the people who are in these programs ultimately want a normal life with friends and family who care about them. It's the environments that some of these individuals are being reared is what's detrimental to their development as people. B.A.M gave these individuals what they feel they're missing. This plus our strict enrollment policy enables them to accomplish goals they set for themselves."

"In your opinion, why haven't such a seemingly progressive program received the funding needed to expand?"

"That's the question that puzzles our entire organization. We have sought help from the Federal Prison Board for the last two years with no success."

"Hopefully, this year will be different. If you want more information on B.A.M or if you want to volunteer you can log on to www.bam.com to find out more information."

Mr. Chaney bitterly said, "Now do you understand my predicament."

Jokingly, Mr. Gaviston responds with his Texas humor. "Yeah, it seems to me like this boy and his organization is doing your job for you."

"Real funny Samuel, I need you to find out as much as you can about Jurist Johnson's past, present and future."

"I got you covered. Frank, I'll have everything you need to know about this guy in about two weeks. I'll call down and put one of my special teams on it when I get off the phone."

"Thanks Sam, I knew I could depend on you."

"No, problem old buddy. Is there anything else I can help you with?"

"Nall, that's it. Just send whatever you find to my office."

"Will do," Mr. Gaviston said, as he hung up the phone, and called his special unit.

Meanwhile, as they're riding to back to the office Jurist and Isis talk about the meeting.

"Jurist, do you think that they're going to approve the program?"

"Honestly, No. It's not in the Prison Board's interest to rehabilitate. That's the job of the community."

"Did you ever think that they would?"

"Nope! Not once."

"Well, why do you do it? If you see these people don't care why
work so hard to get their help, don't you want to do something else
with your life?"

"Yeah, I want to hang out with my family, enjoy life and not have to
worry about fighting for others. But until that day come, my job is
to be the watchman on the wall."

They stop talking, and just ride for a second. Then after some
deliberation Jurist said, "Hey Isis, I'm very grateful that you
continued to stand by me especially through, you know, my hard
times."

Isis smiled at Jurist, flattered but a little stunned, "I believe that's
the nicest thing you've said to me in five years."

"I know I can be a little over barren at time."

Isis cuts in, "And bossy and arrogant."

Jurist cuts her off, "All right, all right now."

"I'm sorry, go head. Now what were you saying?"

"I was saying I'm going to drop you off so I can go to the office, and
get some work done."

"I can never win with you, ha Jurist."

"That's not true. Believe me sister; stick with me, and in the end we
will all win."

After dropping Isis off, Jurist goes back to his firm. As he sat at his
desk he looked at his watch, and noticed that the time is 3:59 p.m.
Jurist pulled out a photo of him and Isis, and stared at it for a

moment then seconds later the phone rang; Jurist put away the picture, and answered the phone.

"Hello, Jurist Johnson speaking."

"Jurist this is Omar. It's about to begin. They will be by tonight to bug the office, and they're going to bug your apartment tomorrow."

"Alright"

"We have reached the point of no return. So, I hope you're ready."

"I better be."

"Hey, by the way, great presentation today."

"Isis did most of it. "Hey, how did you find out about the presentation?"

Omar responds jokingly, "If I told you I'd have to kill you. But for real, you and Isis make a great team. You always have. Isis is a good woman. A man in your position needs a good woman by his side."

"What you trying to insinuate Omar?"

"Nothing! I'm just saying if you ever wanted to date Isis, nobody would doubt your intentions."

"Omar, when will you ever learn, two single adults can be friends without making the relationship sexual. If anybody should know that by now you should. Isis and I always have been, and will continue to be just friends."

"All right, all right I just want to see you happy."

"If you really want to see me happy, you'll come, and take care of this paperwork I have to finish."

They both chuckle and laugh over the phones.

Teasingly, Omar said, "Now that's you responsibility".

Jurist fires back, "You're in this battle too old man."

"Yeah, but you're the HNIC," Omar said as he stopped chuckling, and became serious, "Jurist remember, they can't stop you from being what you're destined to be. Did your mother ever tell you the true meaning of your name?"

"No, she never mentioned that it had a meaning." Pharaoh use to always say that he might be the descendant of Anthony Johnson, the first freed black slave in America. And then my father told him that the root word of Johnson was John which means favored by Jehovah. Isaiah was a prophet, and he foretold the coming of a child that would lead the people. Jurist simply means knowledge of the law. Which Pharaoh thoroughly believed everyone should know. So he named you Jurist Isaiah Johnson, which doesn't make a lot of sense if you read it left to right. But if you read it, right to left it read, Johnson Isaiah Jurist, (The first slave son favored by Jehovah shall lead them with knowledge of the law).

Jurist responds, "Man, that's deep. But the strangest thing is that I wrote about the meaning of my name in my 8th grade black history paper. And what's even stranger is that it was told to me in a dream by a man who I assumed to be my father."

Before getting to sentimental Omar said in a cracked voice, "Progress through Knowledge." Jurist answered, "Prosperity through Freedom."

Jurist hung up the phone, picked up the papers off his desk and put them in a folder. The name on the file is Ermine Brown.
Jurist looked at the folder and said, "I haven't forgot about you old friend."

Jurist walked out of the office with the folder, unaware of the fact that a sheet had fallen to the floor on the side of his desk.

Chapter 43
Chocolate City

ALTHOUGH JURIST HAD STARTED A LOCAL B.A.M
CHAPTER IN D.C., it had nowhere near the support or recognition
that B.A.M had in Florida. In D.C Jurist had a couple dozen
members working to establish a strong connection with the
community, and found out what the needs of the community were.
In comparison B.A.M chapters in Florida had thousands of
members, and Jurist had already won the hearts, and minds of
many small towns and major cities. The most appealing function of
B.A.M was its support of the people. In five major counties B.A.M
had purchased major housing projects. Reclamation homes were
what they were coined. They provided homes to families who did
not own homes. The members of the families signed contracts.
And when I say everybody in the family signed a contract I mean
everyone; even the children. Families living in the homes
committed themselves to volunteer work in exchange for free
housing. The children were mandated to go school, and participate
in some sort of school activity. Women and men who thought it
would never be possible to own homes flocked to the communities.
B.A.M also had its own security company in which many of the
members were former prisoners and members of the prison

program. They ensured that there would be no violence and/or drug usage within the communities. The rules of the community were strict, and violating certain restrictions was costly. Take for instance littering, three littering charges in a month would get a family expelled from the 15 year program, and they would lose their home, and have to leave the community. Some critics thought that these sorts of penalties were too strict, but Jurist felt that it instilled community value, which helped strengthen family values. This type of community governing provided added incentives for them as well, since most of the workers got paid to protect their own neighborhoods. Majority of the prisoners took their careers very seriously. Mostly because they did not want to lose their jobs or their homes, so they worked diligently. In addition, each community had warehouse stores were they could purchase or order everything from potatoes chips to furniture. As B.A.M members built additional homes, the waiting list for homes were seemingly everlasting. Critics such as Saul the former B.A.M president vehemently stood against Jurist, and the direction in which Jurist was leading B.A.M. He argued that Jurist was a Socialist, and connected with Socialist and Communist rather than Capitalist. In spite of all the criticism, Jurist and B.A.M continued to gather community support.

After Jurist appeared on the news a young rebel named James Jetson, President of the Progression of American African Group, researched Jurist, and all the worked he had done in Florida. Therefore, he contacted Jurist, and scheduled a meeting with him, and a couple of other collegiate groups located at various universities in the D.C. area. Subsequently, Jurist granted them a private meeting to work out the details of Jurist speaking a rally they were holding regarding gentrification. After providing James with all the information he needed. Jurist flew to every Black Action Movement chapter, and made them aware of what was to begin. He advised them that the threat of being watched by the government had become a reality. Jurist provided strict guidelines about contacting him, and new assignments to rally community support for the Black Action Movement. Jurist visited every Reclamation Community, and gathered prayers from the elders. Upon his return, Jurist presented this speech to the citizens, students, and faculty that were present at the university.

"We must take one step a day towards the reclamation of not only our imprisoned brothers and sisters we must take a step towards our culture as well. We have to get out in the community, and let the people know that the revolution has begun, and that their help is needed. No longer will we strive to struggle in a country that promotes divisiveness and refuses to acknowledge it. We must recognize that our lives will continue to be at the mercy of the military, corporations, and politicians that figure head this nation we live in and under."

Applauds started to pour in.

"Thomas Jefferson once said, 'During the contest of opinion through which we have passed, the animation of discussion, and of exertions has sometimes worn an aspect which might impose on strangers unused to think freely, and to write what they think, but this being now decided by the voice of the nation, announced according to the rules of the constitution, all will, of course, arrange themselves under the will of the law, and unite in common efforts for common good. All, too, will bear in mind this sacred principle, that though the will of the majority is in all cases to prevail that will, to be rightful, must be reasonable; that the minority possess their equal rights, which equals laws must protect,, and to violate which would be oppression.' The Federal Prison Board has time and time again lent a deaf ear to our voices, and the government's positions have been oppressive to the meek. That's why we as a people must help this country become a nation that promotes a culture we can be proud of, not one that only speaks of individual achievements. We have been healing this country for hundreds of years teaching it how to love. We need communities that are equipped to handle the illnesses that afflict our people due to the hundreds of years of oppression. Every physician is taught that no treatment plan can be successful if the patient continues to dwell in an unhealthy environment. The patient must therefore be removed from that house of illness and relocated to a healthier environment until that house can be reconstructed, and made suitable to rehabilitate. We have asked the health department, the financial institutions, the housing authority, and the prison board for our last favor. No more will we ask for such weak gestures of friendship. How long must we wait? I'll tell you, no more! We've waited patiently through slavery, black laws, de facto segregation, de jure segregation, and the so-called civil rights movement. Yet still, the people that run this nation continue to practice a relationship based upon despotism instead of democracy towards the economically challenged. Feudalism is no longer the relationship we want to share. By no means does our movement have anything to do with dislike or hatred towards any race of people. We are simply trying to improve our position within the world. I only hope that we are given the opportunity to utilize this freedom that we proclaimed to have. On Aug 28th all B.A.M members, and affiliates will meet at a Sovereign Nation conference in Washington, D.C. to discuss the position we hold as a people, and ways to eradicate the problems in our communities across the nation. All decisions made within this meeting will be made public the day of, and effective immediately. This collective group of scholars, economist, media moguls, and political scientist, will look at the position of our people as an entity autonomous from that which has alienated us, in order to configure the blueprint for a bar of equality linking our Nations. Thank you all for inviting me, God bless America, God bless Africans."

The crowd erupted with a standing ovation. The roar of applause could be heard across the campus. This February 28th was surely a day to remember for Black History month, one reporter that was present wrote. As the applauding slowly silenced Jurist walked away from the podium, and began talking with Isis as he shook the hands of people that walked by. Exiting out a side door through a minimally occupied hallway, they walk out the building, and straight to his car. Jurist said to Isis as the walk, "I have to make another flight out tonight. I need you to obtain a tape of tonight's speech, and send a copy to every major city, and capital city newspaper, radio, and television station."

"You know this is going to bring a lot of bad publicity our way."

"Sadly, that's the only attention that brings about change for our people."

"Jurist, you know I see you like my brother, and for the most part I have never doubted the choices you have made for yourself or for the movement. But are you sure you are willing to sacrifice your career, and possibly your life for this program, and the reclamation of convicts? Do you think if the roles were in reverse they would do it for you?"

"A while back Shayla asked me a similar question."

"And what did you tell her?"

"It's our destiny. Now, will you please go and get those tapes sent out." He smiled at Isis, with an innocent yet confident look in his eyes before he drives off. Jurist heads straight to the airport where a jet is awaiting him. He boards the jet, and meets up with Omar and friends.

Chapter 44
Alliance

I wasn't looking for crack but somehow it found me.
I was just walking the streets when it led me to the heat.
I tried to keep clean so I took it to the sink.
But it forced me to do dirt and sacrifice my ancestor's work.
I often wonder who came to the crib and put crack at our door.
My papa wasn't home and the rent note said get dough.
What a 12 year old kid need a bread house fo.
Still remembering homies saying run yo mouth slow.
Back then the only thing I use to run was my mouth,
Now I'm running every street on the south.
Side of the block, stacking bread in sweathouses.
At the same time summer heat had me forgetting colleges.
Just to keep cool I did things people couldn't have understood.
I'm a player, hustler, thug brought up in my mama's mama
neighborhood.
Now I'm in this prison visited by rotating demons.
Constantly telling me I was breed from no good semen.
But Seaman in the Navy never saw war like this.
Because they didn't have to live a life that reminds them that they
don't exist.

Except for when you need me to come and snitch on a friend.
Damn, I knew that you would come back again.
All these years of reminisce.
Now I know who put the crack in my existence.

WHEN JURIST BOARDED THE JET, he was pleased to see Mr. Sharrieff was aboard. They greeted each other with traditional conversations and grips ensuring one another that they remain faithful to the cause. Jurist digressed and began to tell them about James Jetson. He described James as a person with an old soul and new functionality. As Jurist continued to ramble on about James, Professor Conan was compelled to remind Jurist that there were more pressing issues that needed to be addressed. All the same, Professor Conan made a mental note of the enthusiasm Jurist had for this young brother who had earned Jurist's admiration.

"You're right, we do. So what do we do now? About the Prison Board I mean."

Professor Conan responded, as he took a sip of cognac, "We wait. We wait for the Federal Prison Board's answer and we wait for the conference in D.C."

Meanwhile back in Washington, Jr. Lieutenant Williams has just delivered a package from Director Gaviston's special task force to Deputy Director, Chaney. After being made aware of the fact that a package has been delivered to his office, Mr. Chaney walked to his office and found the video tape. He walked over to his VCR put the tape in and press play. The tape is a recording of the speech Jurist gave at the University. After listening to some of the strong rhetoric used he picked up the phone and called his assistant Katherine Tate.

"Katherine, I just received some interesting information about Jurist Johnson where are you?"

Katherine, sitting on an airplane with a laptop in front of her is looking at a paper file with Jurist social security number on it. As she talks with Professor Chaney she types Jurist's social into the computer, which brings up a complete background history check of Jurist which included everything from newspaper clippings of his father Pharaoh to his involvement with Ermine and statements taken when Ermine was arrested. "I'm following a lead of my own in Florida, she told him."

"Well, when will you be returning? I just received a video from our friend that has me even more concerned with Mr. Johnson and his group."

"I'll be sure to look at it, as soon as I return Sir."

"I'm going to leave it in the VCR of my office. I'll clear you with my secretary so she'll let you in."

When Katherine arrives at the prison where Ermine is incarcerated she is immediately greeted by the warden. "Hello, Mrs. Tate how was your trip?" It was clear to see that the warden was both anxious and nervous about Mrs. Tate's visit to his prison. His voice trembled a little when he spoke and he was very fidgety.

"I don't know yet but I'll remember to let you know before I leave. Now, where is the prisoner, Ermine Brown?" Mrs. Tate's cold demeanor didn't help to easy the warden's nervous either.

"He's in my office waiting."

"Is it safe for me to speak to him privately?"

"I don't know Mrs. Tate. I don't think that it would be a good idea?"

"Is he usually a violent prisoner?"

"No, not really, but he is in here for murder."

While eyeing the warden down, with an arrogant confidence she said, "Give me eight minutes," as she walked in the room and closed the door. Because all of his records state that he is a black male, Mrs. Tate took a moment to hold back her initial shook and surprise of how strikingly white Ermine appears. "Mr. Brown how are you doing, my name is Katherine Tate; I'm the assistant to the Deputy Director for the Federal Prison Board. I know you're wondering why I wanted to talk with you. So, I'm going to get straight to the point, we have reason to believe that you have information about Jurist Johnson that can be useful to us and I'm sure we can make it advantageous for you as well." Leaning back in his chair Ermine responds, "Suppose I refused to answer any questions?"

"Given your situation, I don't think you have any other choice."

"See that's where you're wrong because in here I don't have to tell you anything about anybody."

"I'm sure a couple of months in the hole can change that, but that's not my intention. I only want to know what really happened that night your stepfather was killed and whether or not Jurist was involved in any way."

"Don't you have the report?"

"Yeah, I just would like to hear it come from you. A couple years in prison often help people remember a little better."

"Or forget a little more," Ermine answered back with cynicism. "Besides what do you possibly think I can tell you about Jurist that you already don't know?"

"That's what I was hoping you could tell me."

In the interim, having made it to the safe house in North Carolina Jurist and Mr. Sharrieff are a little inebriated, as they talk about old times. "I must say young brother I'm very proud of you and all that you have accomplished not only for the Black Action Movement but for yourself. It's hard to believe that you have already matured into the man I knew you would become when I stopped to talk to you the first day of my class. I know that somewhere my sister is very proud of you. Mr. Sharrieff told Jurist as he walked across the room to sit near him on the couch.

"You'll never know how much it means to me to hear you say that." They both eventually fall asleep on the couch.

The next morning a couple of Federal Board of Investigation Agents arrives at Nandi's house, and after doing a little surveillance, one of them knocked on the door.

"Hold it," Nandi yells out, "Here I come." Looking through her peep hole she saw the two men in suits so she cracks opened the door, "Can I help you?"

"Yes Mrs. Johnson, I'm agent Anthony and this is agent Bradford we need to speak to you about your son Jurist. May we come in?" He tried to charm and smile his way into Nandi's home but being the suspicious person she is she replies, "No, we can speak right here and may I see your badges and get your ID numbers please?" After showing their badges and providing their ID numbers Agent Anthony advises her that they have concerns that her son is involved with some people who they believe may be very bad company. "Have you spoken to him lately?"

"I haven't seen my son in over a year now. So, what type of information do you need from him?"

Agent Bradford responds, "I'm sorry Mrs. Johnson that's privileged information."

"Then so is mine, good day gentlemen." Nandi gave the agent a fierce look.

Agent Anthony walked towards Nandi, "Mrs. Johnson wait, we still have some more questions for you."

"Too bad because I'm fresh out of answers for you."
Nandi closed her door in his face.

After Jurist wakes up he leaves Mr. Sharrieff knocked out on the
couch. He took a quick cowboy bath, leaves the safe house and
started walking the streets. This was Jurist's first visit to this part of
North Carolina although he spoke at a rally in Raleigh a couple
years back. But this was an unfamiliar part of town and the street he
walked led him to a well known drug neighborhood. While walking,
he noticed a group of young males two blocks away standing on the
corner next to a liquor store. He veers in their direction. As he
walked he surveys the surrounding area. The buildings are half-
empty most of the windows are boarded up and graffiti is sprayed
on many of the buildings. Inside one of the abandoned buildings he
spots a man urinating inside another vacant building. After that he
detected three men and a woman sitting on crates passing around
homemade crack pipes made from a used miniature liquor bottle. A
group of playing kids quickly ran by him and through the alley
between the two buildings where the man was urinating and the
crack smokers were getting high. A police car rides by and Jurist
hears, "Here comes them boys!" When he reached the corner where
the group of young men was standing, he noticed that the volume of
their conversation softened. Their eyes begin to monitor his
movement. One of the guys leaves and walked around the corner.
As he suspects that Jurist might be a cop. Then one of them speaks
to him.

"Hey!" The others are confused by their friend's action, so one of
them asked the other, "What this fool doing?"

Jurist, responds, "What's up bruh?"

The same guy asked, "You not from around here are you?"
His friends contest him for speaking to Jurist, "Man, you don't
know that man. Mister don't pay him any mind. His mama still got
him trying to find his daddy so he just trying to make sure you're
not him. The others in the group start laughing and giving each
other dap.

But the guy (whose name is later found out to be Clyde) doesn't take the joke in stride. He fires back, "Nigga, yo mama the one that got the clinic backed up with mutha fuckers taking blood test to trying to find yo daddy."

"Boo, boo, boo," the others don't find his comeback joke as amusing. Enod a smart young man who decided to drop out of college after he got a couple marijuana charges; whispered to the others, "Hey man, that nigga look just like Jurist Johnson. Don't he?"

Devon a condescending thug who has lived and breathed street life since birth responds, "Nigga, who the hell is Jurist Johnson and what the fuck would he be doing down here this time of morning if he not the police or fiend? And he don't look like no fiend."
"You know man, the nigga that got that prison program in Florida. He was on the news the other day talking about black people coming together. I wish it was J.J. I'll take my ass right with him. Straight to the monument just to tell those crackers to kiss my ass, we want our own shit."

"Ya'll ain't gonna do nothing but stand on this corner and talk shit. Man them crackers ain't gonna let us get shit. They'll blow this bitch up before they let us have a piece of anything. Shit, you see how they treat them Haitians. Every time they catch they ass they send them right back to Haiti."

Clyde jumped back into the conversation, "My mama them say they fixin to go to the conference. They say it's to try to start a network of black people and groups that want to have their own."

Devon counters, "Ya'll can take ya'll I have a dream ass up there if you want to, I'm gonna stay my black ass right here. Them crackers ain't gonna let a nigga do nothing but work for them. Ya'll actually think they care about y'all marching, shit y'all dumber than I thought. Look how much money they about to make when they raise the prices up in all the hotels, just like they do for Beach week

225

because too many niggas in town. I tell you what bring me back a T-shirt, THREE X nigga.

"See that's why nigga's can't get anywhere now," Clyde retorts, "We always looking at the down side of getting together. Niggas too scared to try."

"Nigga we ain't scared of them crackers we just know them crackers ain't wit giving away nothing. Don't you see they stop giving away cheese," Devon continues to make light of the subject. And he succeeds because they all start to laugh, even Jurist chuckles a bit. "Man, them crackers feel they done worked too hard for this shit. First they had to kill damn near all the Indians to get this bitch. Then they had to go all the way to Africa to pick our black ass up to work for them."

Enod brings a little seriousness back into the conversation, "I just want to see what they going to try to do. I want to try to be about something positive again."

"Nigga, the only thing you going to be positive for is an HIV test," said Devon, as he began laughing again. "But seriously though, I say fuck it. I don't think them niggas any better than those crackers. Shit them type of niggas be the worst niggas because they just trying to be like them crackers. They don't care about what we going through. Once they start making a little bread they act worst then those crackers. The only time you'll see them cracker ass niggas is when they coming to get some soul food or buying some dope. Just like them crackers. Shit they even escort them crackers down here like they got some type of ghetto pass."

Enod intercedes, "But I tell you what though. When the field slave gets educated and don't want to go and work in the house anymore. That's when the revolution will start."

Jurist who has been listening from the sidelines addresses the group, "You brothers seem to have a lot of anger built up inside you all. How about y'all come with me and speak about the problems y'all see day to day."

Although Devon had just recently sat back down on his crate, he stood up, as Jurist addressed them, "Come with you and go where. Nigga who are you?"

"To the conference," Jurist responds.

"See I told y'all. You is Jurist, ain't you," said Enod?

"I tell y'all what. Suppose I was Jurist Johnson and I invited y'all to come with me to the conference, would y'all come?"

With excitement Clyde responds, "Hell yeah."

Jurist asked them, "How much time do y'all usually spend on the corner chillin?"

Clyde, now convince that the man they are talking to is indeed Jurist, said "Damn, Cuz he is Jurist Johnson."

Devon refusing to let his guard down fires back, "I don't care if he was Dick Johnson. Shit, ain't none of them mutha fuckers doing anything to help us."

Paying some attention to Devon's distrust, Jurist approaches them again, "I guess it's safe to assume, y'all know pretty much everything there is to know about what happens around here."

"Yeah; If it happens in the streets!" said Enod.

"I tell y'all what; I'll pay y'all one hundred dollars apiece to be my ambassadors to y'all town today."

"Fuck that, make it three hundred dollars apiece, otherwise I can stand here and make that," said Devon.

Jurist squints his eye and looked at Devon, as if he was crazy, "Hell nall, but I tell you what. If you come with me we can talk about what ya'll think we should do to help brothers like yourselves get off these corners."

Enod and Clyde both say, "Bet," meaning that they are in agreement. But Devon remains stubborn and said, "I'm cool, y'all fools go ahead. I'll sit here and get it how I get."

Jurist, Enod and Clyde leaves the corner while Clyde began telling stories about the town. Less than a 100 yards away Jurist saw a lady standing in front of a church preaching with a microphone in her hand.

The woman is reading Psalms 137, "By the rivers of Babylon, there we sat down, yea we wept, when we remember Zion. We hanged our harps upon the willows in the midst thereof. For there they carried us away as captive required of us a song; and they that wasted us required of us amusement, saying, Sing us one of the songs of Zion. How shall we sing the Lord's song in a strange land? If I forget thee, O Jerusalem, let my right hand forget her cunning. If I do not remember thee, let my tongue be cleaved to the roof of my mouth; if I prefer not Jerusalem above my chief joy.

Remember, O Lord, the children of Edom in the day of Jerusalem; who said, Rase it, rase it, even to the foundation thereof. O Daughter of Babylon, who art to be destroyed; happy shall he be, that rewardeth thee, as thou hast served us. Happy shall he be, that taketh and dashes thy little ones against the stones."

Chapter 45
Above and beyond the call of duty

UPON HER RETURN TO WASHINGTON, Mrs. Tate stopped by Deputy Director Chaney's office to review the tape he left for her. She asked Lynn, Mr. Chaney's secretary, "Is the Deputy Director in?"

Lynn said to her, "No, he isn't but he gave me instruction to let you in and to tell you to press play." "Here let me open that for you." "Excuse me Mrs. Tate, (Lynn whispered to her, "Before you go in would you mind watching the phones while I go to the ladies room?"

Taking offense to the question, Mrs. Tate viciously responds, "I will do no such thing, there are many more important jobs that a woman such as myself can find to do other than answer phones; not for you or anyone else."

Immediately Lynn apologized. "I'm sorry ma'am your right."

"And will you please refrain from calling me ma'am!" You're not in your little country town anymore we don't call career women ma'am. For now on you will refer to me as Deputy Assistant Tate. Are we clear?"

"Yes ma'am. I mean Deputy Assistant Tate."

Deputy Assistant Tate goes into the office and sat behind the desk of the Deputy Director. She uses the remote to turn on the TV and VCR and began watching the video footage. Before leaving to go to the restroom, Lynn forwards the calls to the Deputy Director's office, thus the phone rang as Mrs. Tate is watching the video. The phone rang a couple of times before she finally decides to be inquisitive and answer it. "Hello, this is Deputy Director Assistant Tate speaking."

"Hi there Mrs. Tate, this is FBI Director Frank Gaviston. I need to speak to Director Chaney."

"I'm sorry Director Chaney isn't in, can I be of some assistance Sir?"

"No, but what's the fax number over there."

"Area code 240-555-1212"

"I'm going to fax some important information over to you all. I need you to make sure that Director Chaney receives it as soon as possible."

"No problem Sir."

They hang up the phone and Mrs. Tate goes back to watching the video. A minute passes and the fax arrives. Mrs. Tate pause the video and walked over to the fax machine. She began to read each page as they come in.

"Director Chaney, I seriously suggest that you carefully consider the ramification of accepting the proposal of BAM for joint collaboration with the Federal Prison Board in regards to the Minority and Economically Challenged Prisoner Program. We have reason to believe that BAM is sponsored by an extremely wealthy group of minorities yet to be identified. My people perceive that Jurist and his group can be a bigger threat than Malcolm, Martin, or the Black Panther Party could have ever been. Our sources have revealed that there are BAM associated organizations across the nation. Jurist has the allegiance of hundreds of organizations large and small. As of right now, Jurist's whereabouts are unknown but we will find him undoubtedly. This is a very sensitive matter that needs to be discussed amongst the upper divisions of national security before you give them a definite answer. If we don't handle this matter with extreme care we could be facing a full-fledged racial uprising. Close to a million people are expected to attend a conference held in Washington D.C on Aug. 28th. Our sources revealed that this conference will be the beginning stage of a nationalist movement. A meeting like none we have ever seen in America."

Soon after Mrs. Tate read the letter, Deputy Director Chaney called her on her cell phone. She advises him that Director Gaviston called but declined to advise him of the information he received via fax. She immediately began bombarding him with information she gathered from Florida. Within the conversation, they decide to decline the proposal based on a lack of federal funding allotment and due to the fact the organization does not present a clear mission of the organizations purpose of the program. The next day Deputy Director Chaney's secretary Mrs. Lynn intercepts a call from Director Gaviston.

"Yes, this is Director Gaviston I need to speak to Deputy Director Chaney."

"Hold one second please." She places the call on hold and called in to Mr. Chaney's office. "Director Gaviston is on line one, Sir." Mr. Chaney sets down his cup of coffee and informs her to patch him through.

"Sam and I were just about to contact you. I received your fax but my Assistant and I had already sent off the denial letter. Mrs. Tate has a hunch that Jurist had more of a hand in a murder case involving a friend of his. Besides Sam you can't possibly believe that these organizations pose a serious threat."

"Did you not receive my fax from the other day?"

"Yes, but you are talking about a bunch of community service organizations and college students, they have no military training and no attachment to their past culture. Most of these people are materialistic and egotistical and are only members of these organizations to promote their own fantasies of grandeur."

"Be that as it may, I have the responsibility of protecting this nation of any and all threats and I see this Black Action Movement as a direct threat to government power and we want to use this prison program of theirs as a bait to infiltrate and gain more information about the true leaders. Jurist isn't the one running the show, there are others and we intend to find out who they are. I have to inform the National Security Advisory Board what has happened and locate Jurist fast before it's too late."

In the months to come, Jurist remains at the safe house in North Carolina using throw away phones and video tapes as a means of communication. BAM designated speakers travel all across America to promote what they had coined the Re-Soulution Conference. The Council wanted to spread the message that this movement had nothing to do with civil rights and liberties that people already deserved to have. This movement is about the deterioration of the Soul of the Black community and what the so-called leaders of the Black community were going to do about it. There were meetings, rallies and seminars being held weekly in every state showcasing the successes BAM had in Florida under the leadership of Jurist Johnson. People were astounded to learn that there were communities in Florida in which hundreds of families and ex-convicts were living in virtually crime free neighborhoods, with stores, schools and jobs for everyone able to work. BAM also had infomercial running in forty-two states explaining BAM's mission, spotlighting Jurist leadership, providing footage of past speeches Jurist had made and specifying the importance of uniting in Washington, DC on August 28th. Many people by then had heard of Jurist but the infomercial gave them an opportunity to get a firsthand look at what he accomplished and how he did it. It was as if Jurist was running a presidential campaign. The Supreme Council authorized millions of dollars in advertising which went through BAM and to predominantly Black advertising firms. Everyone fell in love with Jurist's charismatic approach to change. And, when Jurist was able to produce the proof that his program was denied twice; it fueled the fire of disbelief that the America government had no intentions of helping African-Americans or any other minority and economically deprived individual.

Chapter 46
Cocooned

AUGUST 28TH 4:05 A.M. Jurist is at his desk writing a letter to Ermine.

"By the time you receive this letter I will probably already be in jail. I have decided that I'm going to go public and tell the truth. I can't bear the burden of a hypocrite. I don't know how everyone will react to it but my blood father once told me, if I am to be a true leader, I must be willing to fail if I am to succeed. I know that this has been an odd and terrible situation for you. But soon the worst will have come to past and our fates will once again cross paths. All my love and chief joys are with you, my truest friend for if I hadn't known you I would not know myself."

As soon as Jurist finished writing his letter Professor Conan walked in the room.

"Jurist I need you to come with me I want you to meet some friends of ours."

"Omar, I'm five hours away from making the most important

speech of my life. I don't feel like meeting anyone right now. I want to concentrate on practicing this speech."

"That's exactly, why you need to get up and follow me."

Jurist and Professor Conan exit the building through a maze of secret rooms and hallways until they eventually reach the street and walk over to this black SUV and get inside.

Professor Conan began introducing Jurist to the men inside the truck, "Jurist, I would like for you to meet Chief Nightingale, Chief Campbell and Chief Plymouth. They're members of the Native American Tribal Council."

Jurist quickly realizes that Professor Conan has something big under his sleeves and he is eager to find out what's going on. Jurist has long ago voiced a strong reverence for the Native American people and the success and failures of tribal villages. "It's a pleasure to meet you all."

Professor Conan knowing Jurist's enter most feelings regarding tribal and sovereign life planned a meeting with three of the most influential tribal men in the Native American communities. "Well, I need to go and make sure everything's okay. Besides you all have a lot to talk about."

"Omar," Jurist softly utters. Then Chief Nightingale intervened. "No need to worry Jurist let me explain to you who we are and what we represent. I represent the Chique tribe in Pennsylvania. Our tribe owns several resorts and casinos in northern Pennsylvania. Omar wanted...."

After spending about four hours of heartfelt conversation and negotiation with the Native American Tribal Council; Jurist is about to make his way to the podium amongst the hundreds of thousands of people who showed up to make their stance for nationalism. Chaotic cheers are heard for miles as Jurist stood in front of the microphone.

"Thank you, Thank you. Progress through Knowledge"
The crowd responds in a massive roar, "Freedom through Prosperity."

"Before I came to speak with you all today, I thought long and hard. I mean I really tried to get in touch with my inner most feelings regarding my lack of interest to fully assimilate into the US conception of America and all it entails. Nevertheless, I realized that the overwhelming obstacle was my own fear. I fear America not for what it is but for what it was and what it isn't. I feared the leaders of America and I didn't just acquire this fear recently, I acquired this fear early in life. It was transferred from my father and injected into my conscious, as rapid and fatal as a bullet; just as many sons and fathers and mothers and daughters before us. It's as though the darkness of the past continuously leaks into the present and future plans of people of African descent not only in America but other countries as well including the Motherland herself.

"I wondered constantly, was it really the white race that brought forth such distrust, disbelief and dissension amongst the African American people. Can we successfully prove that through no fault of our own, White people are directly responsible for the institutional afflictions suffered by the Negro? Or could it be that disunity was so inbreeded into the lives of our people that we now use the nooses of yesterday to choke one another today? Or is today simply yesterday in living color instead of black and white?

"Whatever the reasoning, my question is why have we not banded together? And to everyone who feels that I am trying to create a war, I only have this to say: Imagine yourself at the first war that was ever fought with the only loaded gun in the world in your possession. What would you say or do to stop the people involved and most importantly the agitator. Well that's my job, right here, right now. I would like nothing more than the opportunity to stop this four hundred year war and develop a plan that will allow all parties the opportunity to coexist in peace. And believe me I do want peace, but I also want and will have liberation. Many people want me to preach hate and make racist comments so our worlds will continue to collide. The fearful nonbelievers insist a coexisting diverse community will never work. Why should we want our own? "Life as we see it is good here. But that's the oppressed mentality that our people have had to fight against since the first slave sought freedom. Nevertheless, our fight can't solely rest upon the premise of black freedom through white hate. Our fight must include all humanity for we need a home within the perimeters of land we share, a place to heal the souls of our people and rejoice in the joy of our emancipation; one which does not alienate us from our accustomed way of life. We need and want alimony from this arraigned marriage. My magnanimous goal is to be the best friend I can be to as many people as I can. So I ask you now America. Am I your friend? Are we your friends? Or are we still your slaves? If not, on this day, let freedom really ring true and not remain an unattainable dream." Deafening roars of cheers are carried around almost the entire city of Washington.

"Because I trust that if you were in our position, you would make the same decision and choice as we have made. We've tried politics, let's try friendship. As a community or nation, let's reflect upon the amity and camaraderie of the Mere Kat that knows that their protection is gained through their association with one another. With all our technological advancements, we have yet to find a solution for this continuous regression of human civility. We see that the world we live in is merely the projection of an elitist perception and this elitist perception has been and will continue to be our reality unless we put an end to it now. For centuries, the elitists have waged a united war against the common workingman and woman. Yet still, we faithfully stood by their side receiving only widespread diseases, poverty, and war. Successfully, we were convinced to abide by laws that they themselves do not abide. Through the art of double-talk, the elitists not only tricked the people of African descent they have deceived all races and nationality including the ones for which they belong. Today, you, my beautiful brothers and sisters are being given the opportunity to truly live in a United Nation. One whose creed is Progress through Knowledge and Prosperity through Freedom."

Suddenly, a ripple of whispers is heard, as scores of Native Americans dressed in their native attire begin to make their way through the crowd and up towards the stage. Jurist quickly calms the crowd.

"Everybody stay calm and do not be alarmed! Our Native American brothers and sisters have come to join us and take their rightful place in this fight for righteousness. Before we can demand apologies (or anything else for that matter) from others, we must first make right the wrongs committed by our ancestors who either aided the English, Spanish, and/or French in their wars against the Native Americans.

"We as Black People and African-Americans must be held accountable for our actions and establish a treaty with the rightful owners of this land. While you all contemplate about this, I want you all to know that this is not the first time African and Native Americans have decided to put aside our differences to work together.

"Throughout our most glorious and tragic history, Africans and Native Americans were able to build communities together where they coincided peacefully and neighborly. In colonial times they were called Maroon communities, but those communities only represent small examples of how Native and African American people coexisted to overcome seemingly insurmountable odds. The African and Native American communities of old became so intertwined that most historical records considered the African and Native American people to be one. This is the type of sisterhood and brotherhood we must rekindle. As a people we were welcomed into the homes and lives of the Native American people. It's only right that we help them gain back what's naturally theirs and not try to fight to gain a piece of stolen property. I came here without a written speech because I wanted to talk to you all from my heart. My god given father once said that 'The best answer is the truth.'

"A lot of times we choose to obscure the truth for our own personal benefits. But if I or anyone else is to become a leader he or she must not keep or prolong the truth. I will not allow a lie to come between us. Instead I'll put my fate and my faith in the hands of my true peers, including our Native American brothers and sisters because I like of lot of you all acknowledge the fact that we got Indian in our family."

The crowd cheers and applauds for about 10 seconds, as Jurist raised the hand of the Native American Tribal Council President.

"Now I have something else to share with you all, something that without the forgiveness of my people I cannot accept any position within this race for true national freedom. When I was a senior in high school a friend of mine came to me for help...."

Jurist quickly flashes back to when Ermine came to his home after leaving the hospital and seeing how his stepfather had brutally beaten his mother.

"I'll put your food up for you. The only thing you can do for him now is pray," said Nandi.

Jurist walked to his room and lies on his bed. Then he noticed Pharaoh's briefcase on the floor beside him. He grabbed the briefcase and pulled out a letter that Pharaoh had written.

Pharaoh's letter:

Words to my First Born

Son the duties of a friend, sometimes goes beyond social, community, state, or national laws, regulations, and sanctions. There are times when a person is called to do something for someone else that they wouldn't rightful do for themselves and a lot of times this is done for the eternal and fraternal love of a friend. For, violating such a valued and honored covenant between two or more individuals bonded by friendship mortal restraint is all but a crime in and of itself. That's why the selection or choosing of a friend becomes the most challenging responsibility a person can undertake. This challenge of acknowledging a true friend is normally offset by mere association with individuals that usually congregate in a frequented location or through routine visual or verbal contact. But by no means can these placid, mediocre associations with routine individuals ever compare or defeat the pure and true sanctity of genuine friendship. I have a friend name David. David is a young man that sacrificed a life of his own, for me. Everything that I have accomplished and attempt to accomplish to better our lives has been a reflection of David's commitment to our friendship. Although our skin colors are as different as the sun and the moon, our purpose is the same, to penetrate the darkest of clouds in the day or the night and provide light for those who are trying to see. So, now it's my turn to pay my debt to not only my friend but my community as well. For, he is a friend who believes in me, in my capabilities, in our cause and in our friendship.

After reading the letter Jurist climbed out his bedroom window and ran to Ermine's apartment. When he got to the apartment he heard some rustling in the back room. All the lights are out in the apartment so he creeps slowly through the living room then he heard Ermine's stepfather, "I'll teach you, for pulling a gun out on me."

Jurist walked in the room and saw Ermine battered and bruised and saw the gun on the counter next to him. Jurist grabbed the gun. Frightened but resolute he yells, "Get away from him."
Faintly Ermine called out, "Jurist!"

Agitated by Jurist interruption, "Boy put that damn gun down now, befo I come over there and beat you wit it."

"Ermine come over here," said Jurist.

Mr. Putnam looked back at Ermine. "Boy, you better not move. And you, you better put that gun down right now before I come over there. I ain't gonna tell you no mo."

Ermine's voices cracks as he orders Jurist, "J, shoot him. Shoot the bastard"

Mr. Putnam looked back at Ermine and points his finger at him, "Boy, didn't I say shut up." Mr. Putnam walked over and kicks Ermine in the side. Ermine grunts and balls up. Then Mr. Putnam started walking toward Jurist. "Boy, I'm tired of playing with you." Jurist screamed, "Stop Mr. Putnam, please stop!"

Mr. Putnam reached for the gun, "Give me that damn gun."
As soon as he gets in arms distance, Pow! was the sound heard throughout the apartment.

Jurist flashback ends, "In my hand I hold, all the information the state needs to release Ermine Brown and imprison me. But before I go to prison I want you all to know that this movement has nothing to do with hate for another race; it's about transcending racial and economic stereotypes. It's about strengthening our communities, educating our children and networking to provide opportunities for those who have no connection to the social elitist. Through the actions of the civil rights movements in the 50's and 60's, we only gained the equality of a lower class citizenship. Now, it's incumbent upon us to redefine social standards and the merits thereof. A separate nation is not what's wanted but a progressively healing nation is what's needed for our people. But until this country is able to reach its full potential, a sovereign nation is what we were forced to become hundreds of years ago."

Shocked by Jurist's testimony, the crowd became as quite as a desert. Then sirens are heard all around the park. FBI agents appear and begin rushing the stage.

Someone in the crowd shouted, "Run Jurist."

Then the crowd started blocking and fighting the police, but before a full blown riot erupted Jurist screamed as loud as he could into the microphone, "Peace."

Then everyone stopped and looked at Jurist, "No, I go in peace." Jurist reached out his hands to be cuffed then he shouted with much conviction his voice, leaning towards the microphone, as the FBI agents escort him off stage, "I demand a jury of MY peers."

Months later at a Washington, DC incarceration unit, Ermine visat Jurist and for the time first Ermine understands the heartbreaking emotions of seeing a true friend on the opposite side of the glass.

"Jurist, bruh I'm sorry man. You know I wasn't going to snitch on you bruh. You know that right."

Jurist unshaved and clothed in a county blue jumper, "I know man, but I wouldn't have blamed you even if you had. I heard they threw you in solitary for two months."

"Yeah man, that Deputy Assistant Tate is a real bitch. She got it in for you man. If I was you, I'll watch my back in here. Never let your guard down, never! I hear she got connections with the Aryans."

"I'm not worried I'm in God's hands. Besides, I only have a week in here to my court date."

"Man, why don't you make bail. Isis told me that your peeps got the money ready."

"Ermine, I did kill a man."

"Yeah, and I served enough time for the both of us. That piece of shit ain't worth all this. He was nothing but a rapist and abuser anyway."

"Bad man or not, he was a living man and I took his life. Hey, don't worry bruh." Jurist smiled, "I told you I only have a week until my trial."

"Yeah, man but you don't know these types of people like I do. It ain't nothing but demons and goons that live behind these walls and the court system is even dirtier than them."

"I don't even want to talk about it anymore. You know what I do want to talk about."

"What?"

"You and Isis; I heard ya'll went out to dinner the other night. You know when you were locked up she told me she thought you were cute."

"Oh yeah!"

A guard walked by, "Visiting hours are up Johnson."

"Hey Ermine, if something do happen to me and things don't work out the way I planned, I want you to take over for me, Isis will help you out."

"Why can't Isis take over? I don't know anything about being a leader."

"Because! I rather have someone out to kill you then someone trying to kill her."

"Hey man that's messed up." They both smiled and laughed.

"I'll see you when I'm free."

Jurist put his fist to the glass. "Progress through Knowledge" Ermine places his fist on the glass. "Prosperity through Freedom" Jurist then turned, and walked away. As Jurist is beginning to walk down the stairs, a short white prisoner with brown hair and glasses walking behind him called his name, "Hey Johnson?"

Jurist turned around. "Suck this, you black bastard." Jurist falls down the stairs and the prisoner ran down behind him and called for help after he gave the knife to another prisoner who walked by.

The prisoner screamed, "Help, help Johnson has been stabbed."

Jurist with blood in his mouth looked up and smiled at the prisoner who has Jurist's blood over his face and hands, and asked him with a joyous look of conviction, "Who do you believe in?"

To Be Continued.....

Coming Soon!

Sovereign Nation

ASCENSION OF THE UNSPOKEN

.

www.ingramcontent.com/pod-product-compliance
Lightning Source LLC
Chambersburg PA
CBHW020617260626
47157CB00003B/1055